THE STRIKER
OF CHOI

JULIE ALSPAUGH

Published by Little Lamp Publishing 2025

Printed in the United States of America

Second Printing, 2025

ISBN-978-1-966775-02-7

This book is dedicated to the children who have grown up believing they are not wanted and do not belong. God has not forgotten you.

"Come to Me, all you who labor and are heavy laden, and I will give you rest."
Matthew 11:28

CHAPTER 1

Mort went on pulling weeds from around his tomato plants, trying hard to ignore the thin boy who had seated himself on the fence rail a few feet away.

"How come you don't like me?" the visitor asked, resting his heels on the rail below where he sat. "You saw me come up."

Mort jerked at a stubborn weed.

"I know you did." The left side of the boy's face was a fading purple. A line of the same color streaked across the right side of his face where a drip of the dye had escaped. The youth adjusted the leather cuff that encased his right wrist beneath his matching purple hand and glanced up at the pale sun. "You always stiffen like you've seen a snake when you catch sight of me." There was a twinge of hurt in his voice.

"Go away, Striker. You're not wanted here." Mort muttered without looking up.

"It's a hot day. I could help you weed." Striker started to slide off the fence but Mort stopped him with a fierce look.

"You stay away from my garden."

Striker climbed back to his post on the top rail and rested his elbows on his thighs. "Tell me the story of when I was born."

"Go curse someone else." The hate in Mort's voice was unmasked.

"If you don't tell me the story, I'll spit in your garden."

Mort glared at him. "I'd cuff your ears if you weren't the

Striker."

"You're welcome to try it." The boy sat up, challenging the farmer with a stare of his own. "The legend tells that the one who inflicts injury on a Striker will bring injury on his whole family."

"Don't spout legend to me, boy!" Mort snapped. "Didn't my best laying hen die last year after my wife accidentally threw the dishwater on you? I know about curses and legends. You're the curse of this town. And heaven knows why a nice town like Choi was cursed with a Striker when according to your uncle there hasn't been one for a thousand years of history."

With his head resting on his palms and his elbows on his thighs Striker had listened to Mort's rant with a bored expression. "Just the same, the story of my birth or I spit in your garden."

A low, unhappy growl escaped from Mort's throat. "One stormy night..."

"Better make it good," Striker warned. "Short stories with missing facts give me a bad taste in my mouth."

Mort sat back on his heels and looked at the eight year old perched on his fence. If he had not been a Striker, the bearer of the town's curse, he would have been a handsome boy. He was well built with rich, tan skin. No other human dared to cut even the hair of the Striker, so the young man had taken to cutting it himself when it became a bother. Short, dark, wavy hair stuck up in all directions from his healthy but lean face. Out of fear, the villagers had agreed that the left side of the Striker's face should be dyed purple once a year. This would erase any chance of the boy being mistaken for a normal child. His right hand was also dipped in the dye at the same time. Thus he was marked as an unwanted outcast.

Now, eight years after he had entered their lives, Striker looked at the town of Choi as his own. His vibrant green eyes missed nothing as he wandered through their little village doing whatever amused him. He was never welcomed into any home or given anything without begrudging complaints. The townspeople knew the health of their town and families depended on the health of the Striker. Striker had embraced his position as the town curse-bearer and had learned to use it at times to his own advantage. So it was that Mort found himself forced to bend to the wishes of the youth perched expectantly above him.

Mort glared at him for a long moment before beginning the story. Striker, more used to glares than smiles, waited patiently. "On a dark, stormy night, a ragged woman stumbled from the Forbidden Forest. She was sickly, haggard, and great with child. In the Forbidden Forest, great dangers lurk…"

"Enough about the woods," Striker complained. "I wanted the story of my birth. You can tell me horrors of the forest another time." There was an impish smile on the boy's face that chaffed the older man's pride.

Sliding his tongue around inside his mouth, Striker looked threateningly at the garden.

"This creature was cursed," Mort went on through clinched teeth. "She was terrified and without the gift of speech. Her time had come to have her child. The townspeople took pity on her, and the nearest family coaxed her into their home. The midwife, Emmery, was called for." Mort grunted as he got to his feet. Moving stiffly, he overturned an empty bucket and sat on it with a tired groan.

Striker made no comment but watched the old man's movements with interest.

"Emmery delivered the child, but when she looked on it, she shrieked with terror. Others crowded around, including Uncle Harron. She looked fearfully at a picture of the crowned prince on the wall, knowing the danger you would bring to him, and then into Uncle Harron's eyes. It was then that she whispered hoarsely, 'He's a Striker!' No one who was there can ever forget the look of fear that came into Uncle Harron's face. In the confusion, no one noticed as your mother took her last breath and slipped from the land of the living. The curse of your coming was already at work. None of us had ever heard of a Striker before. Only Uncle Harron, a learned man, knew the danger your birth had placed us in." Mort gave the boy a meaningful look. The sun was slowly sliding downward. Mort wanted nothing more than to be rid of this nuisance, but he could not afford to lose his crop of tomatoes. The powers of the curse were not fully understood, even by Uncle Harron who stood as the Striker's guardian to protect the town.

Striker rubbed his eye with his fist to hide the wetness of his eyes. "Go on."

"The Striker was one week old when we assembled together to hear the truth from Uncle Harron. He told us the terrible danger we were in. The health of the Striker is the health of Choi. If he goes hungry, the town of Choi will grow hungry. If he is injured, the townspeople will suffer injury. He must be protected at all costs and must never leave the town of his birth. If he were to leave, the curse of the town would be in the hands of strangers. "I know the curse part. Keep going." Striker adjusted his leather wrist guards again with an annoyed expression. If the farmer had been a keener man, he would have seen the pain in the boy's face.

Mort cared little for the feelings of the Striker. His feelings had nothing to do with the health of Mort's family. "Emmery cared for you. She and Uncle Harron were the only ones brave enough to be near you. For the first year, they kept you secluded in the cottage where your mother died. The family that lived there before left the house the very night you were born and moved far from the proper town of Choi. At Uncle Harron's suggestion, your face and hand were marked with the deep purple dye to keep the townspeople from mistaking you for a non-cursed child. Two years later, someone got drunk. The legend had often been questioned and so, when the drunk was challenged, he acted rashly. In his drunken state he took a dare and knocked the Striker to the ground with a rock. The Striker was badly injured. For several days, the health of the town lingered on the brink of death. Uncle Harron brought the best physicians to care for your wounded head. We doubted the curse more when no one in Choi suffered. Two days later, the king himself fell unexpectedly ill. Panic swept through the town, and every resource was used to try to stabilize both the Striker and the king. Thankfully the king's health returned but…"

"And mine," Striker interrupted. "My health returned as well."

"Yes, well, that is obvious since you were the one cursing the king." Mort growled. "Now keep your mouth shut and listen so I can finish and go inside. The king recovered," Mort saw Striker's eyebrow go up and added, "and the Striker recovered. But Emmery disappeared. No one saw her go. Even Uncle Harron had no answer for what had happened to her. The legend was never publicly doubted again."

Swinging his leg over the fence, Striker finished the story. "And the town has been stuck with the little brat ever since." His other leg followed, and he hopped down easily on the far side of Mort's fence. "Thank you."

Mort watched as the boy strode away back toward Uncle Harron's house. Once he was sure the Striker would continue in his course, Mort rose with a grunt and headed inside.

CHAPTER 2

"Here comes Purple Face!" one of the boys jeered as Striker rounded the corner of the barn. Not far from them was the large manure pile used to fertilize the crops. In the hot sun, its smell was pungent and warm.

"Someone said you had something to show me. I came to see it." Striker looked around at the ring of boys. There was not a friendly face among them. Striker groaned inwardly. It had been another trap. Never once had the boys allowed him to join in their games. Yet, prompted by a glimmer of hope that things could change, Striker showed up for their unkind pranks again and again.

Crossing his arms defiantly, Striker disguised his discomfort with boldness. "Well? Where is it? Is the back of a stable all you boys have to excite you?"

Willie Nills moved toward Striker. He was bigger than Striker by about a foot and a half.

"Is there no one your size you could pick on, Willie?" Striker asked in a bored tone. "Or can they all beat you in a scrap?"

The bigger boy kept coming. The others were crowding in behind him, moving steadily toward the eight year old bearer of the curse.

Striker stood his ground despite the cold fear that was welling up inside him. Surely they would not dare to hurt him. Uncle Harron said that hurting a Striker released a curse of pain on the town. Often the curse would fall directly on the culprit. Like Striker, these boys had grown up knowing this, and had seen the truth of it in action. The wall of protection afforded to Striker infuriated the boys his age, and they were always looking for ways around it. Striker knew in his heart that someday the temptation would be too strong and they would actually overpower him. He held his chin a little higher. If they were going to attack him, he was not going to go down without a fight.

Willie stopped just inches from Strikers face. "Plum Boy."

"Is that all?" Striker asked with genuine amusement. Cocking an eyebrow coolly, Striker went on, "That was anything but impressive, Willie. Wait, what's that?"

The boys glanced around quickly.

"I think I hear your nurse calling." Striker's face was smug as he added, "Let me get out of your way so you can run home to her."

Their faces contorted with hot anger.

Willie, without taking his narrowed eyes from Striker, stepped back and held out his right hand. A boy put a rope into Willie's outstretched hand. Stooping, he lit the other end. It flamed brightly.

"You will burn down Mr. Laden's barn, Willie." Striker warned dropping his defiant pose. "Put it out and I will go away. Mrs. Laden is sick."

"Because of you." Willie taunted starting to spin the rope in a circle over his head. "She is sick because of you." He repeated with a challenging glare.

"Fine, I will say it, she is sick because of me. Happy?" Striker stepped out of range of the flame. "Come on, Willie, let it go. You bested me this time. Put it out."

"Aw, Plum Face is scared of fire." Willie jeered.

The other boys joined in eagerly. They were moving steadily toward Striker who was backing just as steadily to avoid the rotating flame. They were moving in like a pack and Striker found it difficult to keep them all in sight.

Willie dashed forward. Striker stumbled and sat down hard in the steaming manure pile. The boys howled with laughter.

"It worked just like you said it would!" They were congratulating Willie, patting his back and looking up to him like he was a hero.

Striker set his jaw angrily. Because of a recent rain, the pile was soggy inside. His hands, pants, and most of the back of his shirt were covered. He did not get another set of clothes until the next dyeing. Angry tears sprung up, but Striker blinked them away. The boys were drifting away, still laughing and slapping each other on the back. Striker pushed himself up out of the muck, his hands sinking deeply into the warm manure. A movement caught his eye. The rope, which had been dipped in some flammable substance, had flickered to life again, and the tiny circle of flame was spreading. Without thinking, Striker scooped up manure with both hands and smashed it around the burning spot to keep the fire from spreading. The second scoop put out the flame. With a sigh, Striker sat back on his heels.

"Trying to burn down my barn?" Laden was towering over him. "Was making my wife sick not punishment enough? Too bad you are too stupid to know that manure does not burn."

Laden and his wife were new to Choi. Mrs. Laden was kind, but there was something about Laden that scared Striker, something hidden and evil that the boy could not place.

"I was putting out a fire someone else started." Striker got to his feet and stood before Laden as a smelly, soggy mess. "I'm sorry Mrs. Laden is not feeling well."

Before the flustered farmer could respond, Striker stalked off across the field.

Striker traveled fast in the heat of his anger. Half an hour later he reached his objective, the swimming hole. Standing at the top of the five foot bank, Striker looked down at the large pool of shining water below. On the far side, the water lapped gently on a sandy shore. Striker did not take time to see the beauty. He was there to pollute the swimming hole with his disgusting self. Moving back from the edge of the jump off ledge, Striker began a running leap as he had seen the other boys do. He was hurtling toward the water at an alarming rate when he remembered that he did not know how to swim.

The surface of the water seemed to have turned to ice as Striker slammed into it with a perfect belly flop. The breath was knocked from his lungs. Flailing in desperation, Striker gasped in a mouth full of water. Panic surged through him as the water closed over his head once more. His lungs burned and he could not find the surface.

A firm hand gripped Striker's arm, and he hurtled upward through the water. It was black now instead of crystal blue. That was the last thought Striker remembered.

"Here's the cursed boy," someone shouted. "Looks like he was trying to drown himself. We're going to have to keep a closer eye on him in the future if we want Choi to stay on the king's maps."

Striker pushed himself to his knees, coughing hard. He looked fearfully at the water. How had he gotten out?

"Up you go now." The voice was joined by others, but Striker did not attempt to discern who was speaking. He was dreadfully tired. His head and lungs ached. All he wanted was to go to sleep.

Suddenly, it registered that the men were touching him. They were going to restrain him again.

"It's not the new year," Striker croaked hoarsely. "Let me go!"

"And have you wander off and drown? I think not. Laden found you trying to burn his barn, and Uncle Harron is looking for you. The king is having a celebration and wants you out of the way so the happiness will last."

Striker looked down at his soaked clothes. "Could I change first?" It puzzled him that there was not a trace of manure on him. Not even under his wrist guards. In fact, the wrist guards were new, perfectly dry leather rubbed soft by an experienced tanner.

"Have you anything to change into?" The speaker's tone gave away his lack of sympathy. He knew what Striker's answer would be.

"No," Striker confessed quietly. "Last year's clothes are too small."

"That's too bad."

"Better make sure he has a new set of clothes lest we all take the curse of his poverty," someone observed from the edge of the search party that had gathered. A murmur of agreement swept through the men.

"If he gets sick, there is no telling what will happen," a gruff voice agreed.

"Why Choi?" a younger man moaned aloud.

"Hush your complaining," the gruff man countered sharply. "No one knows why a peaceful place like Choi got cursed with a Striker. Stop moaning about our bad luck. It has been with us eight years and complaining has not helped yet."

"Mort, your youngest is about the same age as the Striker," Ike's booming voice silenced the others. The men parted as the blacksmith's big, imposing form moved to where Striker was being held. "Do you have anything that would fit him lying around?"

Seeing the protest in Mort's face, the gruff man added,

"It will just be until his things dry, Mort. Or do you want to spend the winter wet and cold this year?"

"I will not have my son in them after that curse has worn them," Mort grumbled as he worked his way out of the crowd and hurried off down the trail ahead of the others.

"Someone fetch the Striker a blanket or two. Let's get him in the cage before the party starts at the castle. We can barely keep track of this living curse and cannot afford a cursed year if he shows up at the castle."

Striker's wrists were cuffed and he followed meekly, his soggy shoes leaking water on the trail as they led him back toward the town. Looking back, Striker wondered again how he had escaped the water's grasp.

CHAPTER 3

Two years had passed since Striker's incident at the swimming hole. The terror of the water and the blackness, along with Uncle Harron's strict warning, had kept Striker far from the water or the cliff above it.

Bored with the usual scenery and hateful looks, Striker found himself wandering the far side of Choi. The soil was poor, and the houses even poorer. Most had moved to the open outskirts of the southern end of Choi to seek better lands for their crops. The cottages that remained were rundown and many of their roofs had long since fallen in. A few days ago, while avoiding Willie and the other boys, Striker had stumbled across the forgotten street. Now, he easily picked his way back to it. The noonday sun shone warmly on his tussled hair as he walked. No one cared where he was. Most of the families would be inside for their meal and would not see him pass. Uncle Harron was at a meeting at the townhouse and would not look for Striker until late afternoon, if he looked for him at all. He would have hours to explore before he was missed.

Striker was pleased with this new find which promised hours of exploration. He wondered vaguely why he had not discovered it before. Thoughts of the cruel boys and the forbidden waterhole crowded into his mind, but Striker dismissed them. He would not let them ruin this new adventure. He was ten now and found himself wandering farther and farther from the little cottage on the edge of Choi where he and Uncle Harron lived.

Pushing against an old gate, Striker discovered that the bottom boards of the gate were buried in the dry soil which refused to give way. It had been years since this gate had been opened. Climbing into the yard, Striker glanced at the old house. There was no sign of life. A smile crept onto his thin face. It would be his hideout! He had heard the other boys talking about hideouts and their secret doings when they did not know he was there. He would have one of his own.

His first obstacle was the door. The door to the cottage was wedged shut like the gate. After a few attempts to open the door using the broken handle, Striker gave it a hard shove. He gasped as the door fell inward with a dull thud.

Glancing around to insure that no one had seen him, Striker slipped inside. It was empty. The floor, covered by a thick layer of dirt that had blown in through the chinks in the dried wood walls, made no sound as he crossed the small room. The spaces between the wall boards also let in a good deal of light, making it an ideal hideout during the day. A little shelf hung crookedly on the wall, having only one nail to hold it up now. He could see where the stove used to stand, and the row of nails, which would have held the separating curtain for the bed room. He stood on the door with his fists on his hips. He would fix it up. He could hide special things here and do whatever he pleased. Uncle Harron did not approve of the trinkets or pretty stones Striker brought home when he was young. Now, he would have a place to keep them where they would not be discovered by the other boys.

Striker knew he could get nails from Ike. The hammer he could borrow from anyone since no one dared to deny him anything. They were too afraid they would be cursed and have to go without themselves. Confident with his new plan,

Striker wrestled the fallen door out of the house so he could lean it up against the opening. He would need hinges, too.

On the outside, Striker surveyed his new hideout with pride. Picking up a dead stick, Striker walked along the deserted trail between cottages. Dragging the stick in the dirt, Striker stopped. With the tip he made several distinct but meaningless lines in the soft earth. If only Uncle Harron would let him learn to read. Striker could not understand how his reading would hurt the town. Striker remembered with a shiver how Uncle Harron's eyes had blazed when he had heard Striker's request to learn. It had been a year ago and Striker had not dared to ask again.

A few more lines joined the others as Striker pretended to write his name. He was winding the stick around to make little craters in the dirt when a delicious smell caught his attention.

Striker's stomach growled. Uncle Harron fed him thin watery soup and a lump of bread for dinner each night, but if he wanted anything more, Striker was on his own. He had quickly learned which families served the best foods in Choi. He would show up on their doorstep just as things were being pulled from the oven and wait with his steady eye on the lady of the house. The farmer's wives always humphed and complained about not having enough for their own families, but the threat of the curse hung heavy, and Striker always left with a portion of their meal. The names they called him were hurtful, but Striker had learned that their unkindness was more bearable than the knot of hunger in his stomach.

Quickening his step, Striker scanned the area for the source of the smell. One cottage, near the end of the sagging row, caught his eye. A little tendril of smoke rose into the air from its chimney. The chimney itself seemed to be teetering precariously on the edge of the thatched roof. Striker paused to look at the sad, weed infested garden beside the cottage.

The few vegetable plants he could see had very little produce on them. The delicious smell wafted through the air once more, drawing his attention from the pitiful garden. Striker knocked on the door and it opened promptly. Before him stood a stooped old woman with gnarled hands and kind, laughing eyes. Her white hair was braided to one side and hung a few inches over her shoulder.

"Come right in. I'm Widow Zina. Sit here, this is my best chair." Widow Zina chattered on as she hobbled over to her stove. "I only have two but this one has four solid legs on it and will hold a growing boy better."

When she lifted the lid, Striker knew that pot was the source of the smell that had brought him there. He licked his lips hungrily. Though he had never seen her, Striker had heard of the widow before. Uncle Harron had forbidden Striker to go near her. Until now, there had been enough to amuse him around the central and southern parts of Choi. Now, however, the boys had grown crueler and the water hole was off limits. Unintentionally, Striker had wandered onto forbidden ground. He wavered, but gave in to his growling stomach.

Widow Zina was very old and some said she was almost blind. Hoping she would not discover who he was until after he ate, Striker slipped obediently into the chair she had pointed out. Out of habit, Striker had been glancing around, taking in the room, from the moment he entered the little cottage. The table, tucked in beside the stove, separated the two unmatched chairs. On the table sat a napkin covered basket with bread like lumps beneath the cover. Hooks on the wall around the stove held various pots, pans, and utensils. A bowl of partially melted lard sat on the old stove where it would be easy to access when needed. All around the house things were set out where they were easy to reach. Striker was not sure if any of it actually had another place to be stored. A bedroom area was to the right of the door, behind the widow's back. A worn curtain hung from the ceiling to conceal it from the rest of the room. It was coming down in several places from pins that held it to the wood above. It was a tiny, run down little cottage with a snug feel inside.

The stooped widow put her hands on the handles of the pot and then looked back toward where Striker sat. "Be a good boy and heft this pot over to the table for me, would you? My back has been aching awfully bad these last few days."

Striker rose and took the pot from the stove.

"I fell, you know, a day or so ago," she went on. "Well, you probably did not know. There, put it on this towel so it will not scorch the wood. My late husband made this table you know." She laughed. It was a thin airy sound that could barely be heard. "I suppose you don't know that either. I've gotten used to talking to myself over the years. The table is plenty big enough for a snug family, only we never were blessed with children." She scuttled around the table taking the wobbly seat across from him.

"Perhaps we should change chairs so you don't fall again," Striker offered.

Widow Zina dismissed him with a wave of her hand. "No, no. Let a weary woman rest once she is seated. You're a kind boy to offer though. I like that about you. I'll hold on while I eat."

Striker waited expectantly. When he joined other families at meal time he was always put on the front step or on the hearth in the winter so he would not taint the family table. But Widow Zina had offered her table without hesitation. Striker was sure she could not see who he was.

Widow Zina folded her hands, bowed her head, and said a grateful word of thanks to the Almighty God for His provision of both the food and the nice young guest to share it with. She looked up at Striker expectantly when she was through. "Do you care to serve the stew? I saw you up the road and made such a big pot hoping to lure you in that I'm afraid I can hardly reach the spoon with these gnarled hands of mine."

Striker sat for a surprised moment before reaching for the serving spoon. How long would this last? He had never been treated like this before. He had lived ten years as the curse of Choi and had learned to push in for food like a young hog would do in order to be fed.

"Heaven's boy, what do you think I am, a giant? I cannot eat that mountain you've served me."

Striker blushed and quickly set down the spoon ready for a tirade of lectures.

"You take my bowl and give me just a scoop in mine," she laughed, pushing it across the table towards him. "I would like to see myself eat all that mountain. It would fill me up right to the back of my throat and there would be no room for pie." She paused to look at him. "What's the matter? There's nothing wrong with this bowl. You're a growing boy and need mountains of food. I'm an ailing old woman and only need a little to satisfy me now."

Uncertainly, Striker took up the spoon and put a tiny scoop into the empty bowl.

Widow Zina laughed airily. "My man used to do that to me too! What fun he was and how he could make me laugh. Now put a decent scoop in that bowl. I'm not a bird either."

Once she was satisfied, Striker slid the bowl to her. "That is more like it. Here, you will want a piece of bread with it."

Striker took the bread. Using his spoon he started shoving bite after bite of the delicious stew into his mouth.

"Young man!"

Striker froze. Juice from the stew slid unnoticed down to his chin where a drip hung precariously.

"Sit up straight and do not shovel that stew as if you

were slopping the pigs. Did no one teach you any manners?"

Striker tried to deal with what was in his mouth, but she was talking again before he was able to speak. He moved to wipe his face with his sleeve but a sharp reprimand from her froze him once more.

"Stop! A sleeve is attached to a lot of fabric and you must go without until the entire shirt is washed and dried. This, young man, is a napkin." She held up a worn but clean piece of cloth that lay beside her place. It is much easier to wash and requires nothing to be taken off that is needed for daily decency."

Ashamed, Striker took the napkin. Wiping his face awkwardly, he glanced over at Widow Zina. Instead of the sharp annoyed look he expected, he found that she was busily fishing a carrot onto her spoon. No one had ever cared how he ate. Good food was hard to come by. Uncle Harron's soups were thin and watery, and Striker drank them without a spoon at a chair in the corner, not at the table with the learned man. Uncle Harron often read while he ate and he said Striker would soil the books if he sat too close. Striker knew by now that Uncle Harron had other reasons to keep his distance.

The widow glanced up with a smile. "That is more like it. It will taste better if it is eaten properly. No need to let it ruin your meal. You can have as much as you please."

"Thank you." Striker found he had to take smaller bites to keep the stew on his spoon when his face was so far above the bowl. The widow was right, it was delicious.

"See now, you are a handsome boy when you are not eating like a pig."

Striker grinned. He liked her frankness. Though her words were sharp, there was no malice in them.

Realizing Widow Zina was studying him, Striker quickly changed the subject.

"Were you hurt much when you fell...the other day?"

"My back is bad anyway and there are very few days when I do not have pain. Would you believe that I tripped on my step carrying in the little sticks I use to keep the stove going? Imagine that. I have been stepping over it for years. Suddenly I go head over heels and the sticks go flying all over the floor." She laughed her quiet, airy laugh. "It would have been a sight to see had anyone been around to see it. There I was, lying on the step, unable to get up." Her cloudy eyes grew sad. "Some day I will not get up, you know. Those are the days I am dreading." She was silent for a long moment. Striker ate carefully, watching her without a word.

With a shrug and a laugh Widow Zina went on, "But I pray the Almighty will take me home to be with Zeke before that happens. If He does not, He will give the strength to carry on until it is time. Look at you, you've endured a lot in your ten years here in Choi."

Striker frowned. "I didn't think you knew who I was."

The widow's smile was kind. "How could I not know? You're famous in this little town."

"I wish I was not. I wish I did not bring a curse. I went by your house a few days ago. That is probably why you fell. But I didn't know you lived here."

Her eyes crinkled merrily and she suppressed her laughter with a napkin over her mouth. "Do you want to know why I fell?" Widow Zina paused to clear her mouth with a drink of water. "I fell because my clumsy foot caught on the step." She laughed again at the thought of herself sprawled on the floor. Seeing his serious expression, she too grew serious. "Young man, you had nothing to do with my falling. Bad things happen because we live in a world with sin. When we broke the laws of the Almighty God at the beginning, evil came into the world. Striker, you're not evil. You're a good boy with a kind heart."

Striker put the last bite of stew into his mouth. Was this

a dream he was having? It could not be real.

"I expect you to visit often after this, but you must not tell anyone you come here. I'm very old, and I remember things that were before the other townspeople were born. This makes some afraid." Her laugh was now familiar and comforting. "But you're a child. You don't understand these things. Only don't tell, and we will have many happy times together after this. Now get yourself another serving, if you like. The sooner we finish, the sooner we will get on to the pie!"

CHAPTER 4

"Something is different about you. What have you done?" Uncle Harron's sudden accusation broke the stillness of the room.

Striker, who had been sprawled out on his straw mattress at the far side of the room, propped himself up on one elbow. "I don't think I've done anything, Uncle Harron. Nothing I am forbidden to do." A thoughtful look came into the boy's eyes. "I did pet that old tabby that lives by Mort's farm." His eyes shone. "Usually she runs away, but she just sat there, and I petted her right on top of her head."

"You are too old for such silly things," Uncle Harron admonished with a strict cock of his eyebrow. "Have you gone to the swimming hole?"

"No, sir. The boys threaten to throw me in, so I am careful to keep away from it as you instructed." Striker sat up, legs crossed under him. "Do you think you could teach me how to swim?"

"Swimming is not a necessary skill. Simply stay away from the swimming hole."

"Oh, you don't know how to swim either." The boy sat back, disappointed. "Surely someone could teach me."

Uncle Harron scowled at Striker. He did not like for his ignorance on any subject to be recognized. "You managed to get out of the water once. Do not tempt fate."

"Do you think I could have a puppy? To keep outside

of course."

"And if it scratched or bit you and your curse killed it?"

Striker blinked at him. "Must I always carry the curse of Choi?"

Again the dark scowl covered Uncle Harron's learned face. "That is not for us to decide."

"But you were not always educated." Striker knew he was pressing his luck to go on. "You were a boy once and studied hard to learn all the things you know. Could I not study too and learn to be something different?"

"That is outrageous. I will not have you speak of such foolishness again. Do you understand? You are the Striker of Choi. No amount of learning will ever change that. How dare you compare yourself to me?"

Striker glanced nervously at the strong iron ring that was securely fastened to the wall near his mat. "I did not mean to insult you, Uncle Harron. I see now it was a foolish thought."

His statement appeased Uncle Harron who set to the task of stowing his precious books into the chest. He would lock it to keep them far from Striker's prying eyes. Lying back on the mat once more, Striker weighed the things that had been said. Widow Zina said he was a kind boy. A boy who brought life. It had been a year now since he had first met her. Now her garden flourished as Striker faithfully tended and weeded it. Once a week she made a big pot of stew and Striker would make his way, aimlessly, secretly to the door of her cottage. She spoke life and gave him the courage to go on. This is what was different about him. He would have to be careful Uncle Harron did not see the change that was happening inside him. Rolling on his side to face the wall and the dreaded restraining ring, Striker ran through the conversation once more. Was it fear he had seen in the old man's eyes? Was Uncle Harron afraid Striker would find something out that only he knew?

———————

"Hey, Plum Face, finally learned your lesson did you?" Willie jeered as Striker passed their group. They were lounging on the edge of the fountain looking for mischief.

Striker did not respond.

"Nobody wants you around." Another boy threw a stone, being careful it did not actually hit the curse bearer.

His silence seemed to rile them more than a response would have. They had spent the morning cooped up in the schoolhouse and it was still too cold to go for a swim. They jumped at the chance for entertainment.

"My Pa says you killed our milk cow."

Striker stopped and looked directly into the boy's eyes. "I am very sorry. That must be hard for your family."

"So you want to rub it in?" Willie shoved the smaller boy aside. "What did they ever do to you, Plum Face?"

"I apologized, Willie. I don't know how to stop the curse. I only stopped at the Western's farm for a bite to eat. I have nothing against them or their cow." Striker would have walked away but Willie blocked his path. Striker, now as tall as Willie, no longer offered such an easy target.

"Always begging off people." Willie was uncomfortably close. "Can that Uncle of yours not afford to feed you?"

Striker grabbed the front of Willie's shirt. "You leave Uncle Harron out of this, Willie." Striker had no feelings of loyalty for Uncle Harron. Fear of his protector kept Striker from crossing him or allowing others to do so.

"Get off of me!" Willie shoved Striker, forgetting for a terrible instant that he carried the curse.

The boys gasped as Striker stumbled back. The edge of the fountain caught him just behind the knees causing him to fall backwards into the cold water. Had it been anyone else, they would have laughed at the spectacle of a boy's legs sticking up awkwardly from the churning water. Because it was Striker, they stood frozen with fear.

Coughing and sputtering, Striker rose up from the water like an enraged sea serpent.

In his shock Willie had not moved away, and Striker grabbed him once more.

"Let him go, Striker." A voice boomed over them. Neither of the boys had seen Laden approach.

Instantly, they stepped apart. Sloshing out of the fountain, Striker stood shivering, ready to face the lecture he knew would follow.

"If I ever hear you speak a word against Uncle Harron you will get a tanning you won't forget," the burly farmer threatened.

Striker and the other boys blinked in amazement to find Laden was speaking to Willie.

"I'll have your father give you a tanning you will never forget. Uncle Harron is the only one keeping this curse from destroying Choi. He is the only one who knows how to keep that," he gestured at Striker, "from killing us all. You will speak of Uncle Harron with respect, or you will not speak of him at all."

All the boys nodded fearfully.

"Now get out of here. All of you." The last was directed at Striker who stood gaping at the thought that someone would stand up so strongly for Uncle Harron. Never before had he realized how important Uncle Harron had become in the little town of Choi.

Striker turned and ran. As he passed the big storage barn at the edge of the square, Striker heard Willie's voice.

Slowing to a walk, Striker listened.

"I'll make that Striker pay for this if it is the last thing I do!" Willie shouted angrily.

He did not wait to hear more.

The tears flowed unchecked down Striker's muddy face. He did not care who saw them. A stone's throw from where he stood, the townspeople were gathered to bury the only friend Striker had ever had. She was stooped and gnarled in body but she had been very much alive inside. He had gone to her house and found her lying cold and still on the worn wooden floor of her cottage. It was more than he could bear. Running madly from her house, screaming for help, Striker had roused the town. But it was too late. The Widow Zina had gone to be with the Almighty and her dear husband Zeke in the glory. She had spoken of that journey often. Striker had stood by as the townspeople covered her with a sheet from her bed. They would not allow Striker to approach or have any part in laying her to rest. Instead, they had jeered at the widow's foolishness for living alone, putting the blame of her death on the bearer of the curse. How the Striker was connected to her death no one knew, but there was no doubt that it happened because of him.

Now, they were lowering the crude casket into the ground. He was not to approach lest he bring a curse with his presence. So, sobbing from a broken heart, Striker watched them cover with earth the only friend he ever knew, the only one who had seen him as more than a curse.

They moved away, leaving the small mound of freshly turned earth. Striker rubbed his eyes with his grimy hands. He had been working in the garden when he felt prompted to check on her. Widow Zina often said that guiding prompts like that were from the Almighty. Moving forward as if in a terrible dream, Striker knelt beside her grave.

"I am not a curse, Widow Zina. I am a boy who brings

life. I do believe in the Almighty, so I will see you again. If He will give me the strength, I will become what you saw in me. Or I will die trying."

Wiping his nose on his sleeve, Striker paused and gave the grave a sad smile. "I think it might take me a while." Pulling out the handkerchief she had given him, he finished wiping his nose.

"After all," Striker whispered, "it is much easier to wash and requires nothing to be taken off that is needed for daily decency."

Fresh tears sprung up. Striker lay beside the widow's grave and let them flow.

CHAPTER 5

The little boy had been staring across the market square at Striker for some time. When his mother's back was turned, he strode over to where Striker was seated on the edge of the dry fountain.

"Why is your face purple? That part of it, I mean." He pointed to the left side of Striker's face. "My thumb turned purple when I hit it with a hammer. Did you hit your face, is that why it's purple?"

"No, it's purple so you know that I'm a curse and that you should stay away from me." Striker mumbled around the pastry he was eating.

"What's a curse?" The inquisitive boy inched closer.

"A terrible, bad thing."

"Like stealing pastries?" The boy squatted a safe distance from the purple faced youth.

Striker frowned. "He gave it to me."

"No, he did not. I was watching," the boy contradicted. "All he gave you was a sour look. You took it and that is stealing. My mother says so."

Striker shifted uncomfortably. He knew this boy was from the family that lived in the farmhouse that was so far from the town that many said it did not belong to Choi at all. The wind tousled, freckled boy was six years old at most. Perhaps he was the only inhabitant of Choi who did not know of the legend of the Striker.

"What's your name?" Striker asked. For some reason he could not explain, Striker suddenly felt guilty for taking the pastry.

"Micah," the boy responded, glancing back at his mother who was still deep in conversation with the miller's wife. "What's yours?"

Could it be that Micah actually did not know to be afraid? His wide curious eyes were studying Striker's purple hand.

"What would you call me?" Striker did not want to chance awakening some lost memory in the boy's mind by saying his actual, dreadful name.

Micah looked at Striker thoughtfully for a few seconds before answering. "I would call you Javen, because you look like a Javen. Is that your name?" Without waiting for an answer, Micah pointed at Striker's right hand. "Your hand is purple, too."

"I know." There was a twinge of bitterness in the older boy's tone.

"Do you like purple?"

"I hate purple." Striker spat bitterly. He rose and threw the pastry to a goat tied nearby. The owner snatched the pastry from the goat and glared at Striker for endangering his animal.

Coming to stand by Striker at the edge of the dry fountain, Micah peered in. "Why is there no water in the fountain?"

"A boy shoved me into the fountain two years ago when I was eleven." Striker answered carelessly. It stopped that week and no one bothered to fix it since the curse was what stopped it." Striker felt restless but could not seem to pull himself away from this honest, little boy who treated him like a person.

"I like to fish," Micah stated. "You should come fish with me. We live that way." He pointed and Striker had to smile. The boy was clearly turned around. "It's a long way, but you could borrow a horse or get a ride."

"I don't think your mother would like that. It could be dangerous to fish alone with a stranger."

"I don't fish alone," Micah informed him. "My sister Willow comes. She says it's easier to watch me when I'm fishing because then she can read a book."

"Maybe I will wander over your way sometime and see what happens."

Micah grinned with pleasure. Scrambling to his feet, he ran back to his mother to share the good news. Striker slipped out of sight, not wanting to see her reaction.

The long walk had put Striker in a bad mood. It had taken almost a full day to get to Micah's farm. Circling the outer fences, Striker spotted a short stand of trees beyond the fields. Hopping the fence easily, Striker started across the field, walking carefully between the newly sprouted rows as he made for the trees on the far side.

As he had hoped, there was a little stream that cut its way through the trees. Beside the water, sitting on a wide, flat rock, was Micah.

Stopping to look around, Striker spotted Willow sitting up on a rise where she could see her brother below. Her face was hidden by the book she held propped on her knees. The skirt of her faded, floral print dress moved ever so slightly in the light breeze.

Striker went on, moving down into the shallow gully toward where Micah sat.

"Hi!" Micah greeted him cheerfully as if he were expecting Striker. "It took you a long time to walk here. Almost a week!"

"Who are you talking to, Micah?" Willow asked absently without taking her eyes from the book.

"My friend Javen," Micah answered loudly.

"Well, remember to keep your shoes dry while you play. You know how Ma feels about you getting them wet."

Micah rolled his eyes and pointed at the neat brown shoes that sat safely by a tree half-way between him and his sister. "She always says that."

"Have you caught anything?" Striker had tried fishing a few times, but the other boys got upset when he fished at their pool, and further up the river was too shallow for anything but crawdads.

"Nope, but maybe you will bring me luck."

Striker blinked in surprise. All his life he had only brought misery and sadness to people. He hoped his being there would not bring those things on such a nice kid.

"I brought extra string and a hook for you." Micah stood and worked the string from his pocket, while keeping his other treasures inside. He handed it to Striker and plunged his hand in again for the hook. A little cry escaped him. Pulling his finger out carefully, Micah examined his finger. A spot of blood had appeared. Micah bravely blinked back the tears that had sprung up.

"You!" Neither of the boys had heard Willow approach. Now she stood over them her face registering shock and horror. "What have you done to him?" she demanded, pulling her brother against her and farther from Striker.

"He didn't do anything, Willow." Micah pushed her away. "I caught my finger on the hook."

"I told you not to keep it in your pocket." She caught herself and turned on Striker. "You get out of here. You're not wanted. What did my family ever do to you?"

Striker stepped away from them. "I didn't mean to hurt him."

"That doesn't change anything. Go back to Choi where you belong." Grabbing Micah's arm, she propelled him up the side of the shallow bank, snatching his shoes up as she passed them.

"I'll try to come back tomorrow, Javen." Micah called over his shoulder. "I can teach you to fish then."

Striker just barely caught Willow's fierce response. "You will not be teaching that thing anything. Just wait until Ma hears about this. You could have destroyed our crops or killed Pa by bringing the Striker here."

From the other side of the rise, a man watched silently, as the feared Striker sat heavily on the rock where Micah had been, hid his face in his hands, and wept.

———————

Trudging homeward along the dusty road, Striker could think of nothing besides the cool flowing water where Micah fished. His throat was parched. His eyes were weary from scanning the landscape for any sign of water. If he died here on the road, would the town die, too? Striker shook his head to free it from the memory of the rippling water.

His feet were heavy, and his stomach growled angrily for food. Uncle Harron was right. Though he was thirteen years old, he was still just a foolish child. To walk almost a full day without provisions in the heat of the summer was a foolish thing to do. Striker was old enough to know better.

What had he expected? A warm welcome from Micah's family? The child did not know who he was. Was Striker foolish enough to think he could be friends with another child in Choi? Widow Zina was gone and now…Again Striker shook his head. He would not go there. She had died some time ago. He was older now and could read very well thanks to the book she had given him. It was well hidden in the widow's house. He went there often to read or think. The people of Choi said he killed her and was haunting her cottage, but that only made it a better refuge for Striker to read without interruption.

Striker coughed. The dust seemed to be seeping in and drying out his entire body.

He tried again to divert his mind, but it hurried back to his need for water like the leaves he had seen moving over the surface of the brook.

Stumbling, Striker righted himself and scanned the horizon. Nothing green met his eyes. It would be several hours before he reached the edge of the town of Choi. He knew he could not make it. Eyeing the grass, Striker weighed his options. It did no good. He had acted rashly, believed foolishly, and now he must face the consequences.

Stumbling often, he reached the top of the little rise, hoping to see Choi's bell tower on the horizon. Something on the ground arrested his attention. There, in the open road, was a canteen. Beside it lay a neatly wrapped package.

Looking around, Striker saw no sign of anyone. Picking up the canteen, he looked around again. The wagon tracks and hoof prints were all old. No one had passed Striker all day. Unscrewing the lid he took a swallow of the wetness inside. It was cool and fresh. Once his thirst was quenched, Striker's stomach raged more than ever to be filled. Striker stooped and retrieved the package.

"Anyone there?" he called, looking all around. There was no sound except the whispers of the grass and the hum of summer insects. "I'm going to open this package."

Still no sound.

Inside the wax covered paper, Striker found a hearty meal of brown bread and cheese. "If there is no one who will claim this feast I will take it as a provision from the Almighty," he called loudly. To himself he added, "and enjoy it very much," as he sat in the grass by the side of the road. Striker ate the bread and cheese provided. He ate it slowly, enjoying it as he had learned to do at the widow's table. Now that he had given up stealing, his meals were scarcer, and he found he enjoyed what he had much more.

Once he was finished, Striker found his strength was renewed. Stringing the canteen across his narrow chest by its cord, he took to the road once more.

CHAPTER 6

"Marina, look at this," The hushed, confidential tone of the butcher's wife caught her customer's attention immediately.

Marina eagerly stepped up to the meat counter to catch the latest gossip.

"Have you looked at the Striker lately? I think he is looking much thinner. What do you think?"

Marina shifted her basket on her arm and turned to give the Striker a good stare. He was standing alone, gently prompting a toad to jump with a dirty toe.

"Can you see it?" The butcher's wife rattled on, going back to her task of wrapping the meat Marina had requested.

"He's just growing. Both my boys thinned out when they grew last winter. It's a chore to keep decent clothes on those boys. Look at the Striker out there with his ankles sticking out of his pants. It's a disgrace."

Both ladies paused to look at the lean purple-faced youth loitering outside.

The toad hopped out of reach under a rose bush. Striker cinched up the rope that held up his pants and looked around for another form of entertainment. He was unaware of the ladies' probing stares.

"Those clothes are too big for the boy!" The butcher's wife confirmed with a crisp nod of her head. "He is almost all skin and bone. I saw it start a few weeks ago on that especially hot day we had. Imagine it being spring and so hot so early."

"What about him?" Marina prompted gesturing with a thumb over her shoulder at the Striker. She was not ready to let go of a tasty bit of information so easily.

The butcher's wife handed Marina the packet of meat. "Of course I thought, like you, that he was only growing, but I have my doubts."

"Now that you've brought it up, Striker hasn't stolen any of my pies in weeks. Before, I had to make two if I wanted my family to get one."

"Yes, and Keela said he doesn't come by any more to help himself from her garden. All the ladies are talking about it. What a nuisance it was to have him scrounging around and taking whatever he pleased, but now that it's stopped, we hardly know what to do. If the boy goes hungry you know what that will mean."

Nodding seriously, Marina met her friend's eyes. "We will all go hungry."

"Boy, take this, I have no need for it."

Striker looked up in amazement from the meat pie that had been hastily shoved into his hands. The pie was still warm. "Thank you, Ma'am."

Already on her way back to her house, the baker's wife waved him off as if she were shooing a fly.

Striker looked around for a secluded place to eat the prized possession. Not stealing had cost Striker most of his meals, and his stomach growled hungrily. Slinking back between two large bushes on the side of the blacksmith shop, Striker sat cross-legged in the cool dirt. Pausing to thank the Almighty for the meal as Widow Zina had taught him, Striker stuck his purple fingers into the pie and scooped the warm food into his mouth. He groaned with delight. Whatever had come over the baker's wife, he hoped it would stay. Half of the pie was gone when Striker leaned back against the wall behind him with a contented sigh. It felt good to be full. Striker had thought that he would starve if he did not steal, but the Widow Zina was right, the Almighty was able to take care of him.

"A word, Laden." Uncle Harron entered the barn alone.

The big farmer looked up from the harness he was oiling. "What is it, Uncle Harron? You look unhappy."

"The other farmers are complaining. They say you didn't get a good price for their produce at market this summer."

Laden shrugged, "The produce didn't sell well."

"There's talk that you are gleaning from the profit." The older man searched Laden's face for any sign of deceit. The twinge of a smile was all the evidence he needed. "Laden, the farmers will grow discontented. Others will try to go to the market. We are too close to the goal to be careless. Your greed will ruin everything."

Moving the cloth thoughtfully over the leather straps on his lap, Laden spoke in a low tone. "You have the king now, and the power to remove the current rulers."

Though they were alone, Uncle Harron glanced towards the barn door. "We must wait until the boy is of age or Greater Choi will choose another king in the form of an adviser. The kingdom is still unsettled by the tension between the king and Prince Deetry. I have convinced the king not to crown his foolish son. King Deetrian has not yet settled it in his mind that I would be the right man for the position. Can he not see that I am perfect in every way to be the king's adviser and next in line for the throne?"

"Perhaps he is in need of spectacles," Laden muttered.

"Be careful how you step, Laden." The threat was evident in Uncle Harron's voice.

"You make my wife sick again and I'll…" Laden fell silent, clenching his teeth in anger.

"You will what?" Uncle Harron pressed, "You will cut off your only chance at life beyond this lousy barn?"

"Unlike you, I do not have to stay in Choi," Laden pointed out without meeting the older man's gaze.

"Yes, you could become a mercenary again. What of your family, Laden? Would you leave them in Choi? Or take them on your rounds?" Uncle Harron's tone changed. "Have patience, Laden, and you will receive the position and wealth I have promised. It is only a matter of time until I have fully won the king's confidence."

"May I pet him?" Striker asked, looking down at the little spotted puppy that danced and wriggled at the end of Eber's rope.

"No!" Eber pulled the rope, drawing the dancing puppy closer to himself. "You hold the curse. If you touch him he'll die." Eber was a good listener and often repeated what he had heard the grownups say as if it were his own idea. Eber had just turned four. The puppy was his birthday gift.

"I touched Mort's tabby and she didn't die." Striker pointed out.

"Yes, she did," Eber contradicted. "Mort found her dead by his garden."

Striker looked thoughtful. "When?"

"It doesn't matter," Eber answered. "All that matters is that you touched the tabby and it died. You may not touch my new puppy." Gathering the dog into his arms, Eber ran to the safety of the other boys who were playing a game of tag in Fountain Square.

Striker watched them for a while. It looked like a fun game. He knew how to play it but would never be allowed to join. They were nervous and kept glancing his way, so Striker wandered off towards the swimming hole. Swimming was a lot harder than it looked especially because he froze up when the memory of his near death experience came to mind. For years, Striker had avoided the water like it held a plague. But gradually, his curiosity returned and he felt himself drawn once more to its crystal glitter.

Sitting by a tree halfway up the steep side of the swimming hole, Striker waited. It would not be long before the other boys grew tired of their game and came to swim. Striker would watch them carefully, looking for pointers on how to avoid drowning in the deep pool. Two days before, he had managed to flail across the narrow end of the pool without touching the bottom. He felt as if he had swallowed buckets of the water and barely escaped drowning all together, but he had kept his feet off the sandy bottom the whole time. Inside, Striker was proud of his accomplishment.

As Striker had predicted, the boys soon appeared at the top of the leaping point. They were laughing and shoving each other playfully. They swam fully dressed, except for their shoes, because it was a long walk home and the sun would dry their clothes as they went. This started about four years ago as one mother's clever way to avoid doing laundry as often for her rowdy son.

A burst of laughter erupted and someone playfully shoved little Eber who had apparently told the joke. There was a gasp of horror as Eber teetered for an instant on the brink of the leaping point. His older brother grabbed for him, but the little body tumbled unchecked from the edge towards the still water below. The puppy, pulled by the rope after him, cried piteously as it fell after its master.

The scream of Eber combined with the cries of the puppy set the boys into a wild frenzy. In their panic, the boys lost their minds. Instead of diving in after Eber, they ran screaming for help. The nearest farm belonged to Mort. Striker knew the old man was in town today. He had seen him swapping stories with the grocer on his way to the swimming hole. Striker stood. Down below Eber was flailing, desperately trying to keep his head above the water. Without thinking, Striker jumped from the edge. A wave of panic swept over him as he, for the second time, hurtled towards the waters of death. Adrenaline pumped through his body as he plunged beneath the water. Not knowing how he did it, Striker thrashed his way to Eber. The boy's head dipped below the surface and Striker grabbed him. Pulling him up, Striker rolled on his back with Eber's head resting on his chest. The little boy was limp in his arms. Striker sank beneath the surface for an instant. Holding his breath, Striker managed to keep Eber's head above water as he fought for the surface and air. Once again, Striker surfaced. Gasping for air, he kicked hard against the water until he felt the sand beneath him. Rolling over, Striker clasped his hands around Eber's middle and squeezed hard. He had seen Mort do it to a lamb that had frolicked into a watering trough and nearly drown. Water spewed from Eber's mouth. Striker held his breath and heard the boy take a weak breath. Still standing ankle deep in the water, Striker carefully laid Eber on the sand. A whimper nearby drew Striker's attention. The spotted puppy had managed to fight the water and crawl up on the bank nearby. Crouching and whining, it made its way to Eber's side.

Striker resisted the urge to pet the soggy pup. Perhaps Eber was right and it would mean the little creature's death. This was a day of life and Striker did not want to risk hurting the pup. A commotion coming from the trailhead alerted Striker that the boys were returning. Staying in the water to hide his tracks, Striker moved away from Eber and climbed out of the water where he would not be seen.

He watched as the men and boys burst from the woods. Eber's parents were there, tearstained and scolding the boys for being so careless. When she saw her little boy laying on the beach, Eber's mother gave a sharp cry and fainted into the soft sand. No one bothered to catch her. Instead, they rushed to the boy's side.

Striker smiled to see their joy at finding Eber breathing. They praised the little puppy and petted and coddled him as Eber's dad lifted his son in strong arms. The mother was revived with the cool lake water and the rejoicing party headed back towards Choi.

Once everything was quiet, Striker emerged from his hiding place. He had brought life and the joy of it warmed his heart.

CHAPTER 7

"Your hair is wet." Uncle Harron observed coolly the moment Striker stepped through the door into the room that they shared.

"It might have rained," Striker answered casually. The weather was cooler and the sun's strength was weakening as winter neared. This was the reason Striker's thick wavy hair had not dried. He would have to cut it soon if he wanted to continue to teach himself to swim.

"It did not rain." Uncle Harron was in a foul mood.

Striker looked up innocently. "I did not say it had, Uncle Harron. I am sorry I am late. Is there any supper left for me?"

Uncle Harron's eyes narrowed. "You will go without your supper tonight. The town will pay for your impudence."

Striker cocked his head inquisitively. "What is it I have done, Uncle? I did my chores and stayed out of your way today. Have I wronged you in some way? You do not seem yourself."

"I have told you to stay away from that swimming hole," Uncle Harron growled. "I do not like the way you are sneaking around the outskirts of the town. People hardly see you and it sets them on edge." Uncle Harron closed and set aside the thick book he had been studying. "They come to me and complain which interrupts my studying. Then you come sauntering in at any hour you please and are obviously hiding something."

"I am very sorry to have inconvenienced you, Uncle. I was not aware my actions were causing you discomfort. I will stay near Fountain Square tomorrow so you can study in peace."

"You are up to something that is no good." Uncle Harron stood and moved towards Striker.

Inside the teen cringed. He feared Uncle Harron more than anyone could know. Days without food and nights chained to the ring in the wall plagued him even in his sleep.

Uncle Harron touched Striker's hair and the boy flinched. He did not see the hint of pleasure that passed over the older man's face. Despite the changes, the boy was still in his control.

———————————

Striker lay in the grassy field far from Choi. Here no one bothered him and here he could not hurt anyone. For some time he had been aware of someone approaching through the long grass. Striker lay motionless, hoping whoever it was would pass by without seeing him. He had been crying again. Anger and pain mingled into deep racking sobs. A year ago it had happened for the first time after his meeting with Willow. Before, as a child, Striker had often cried when the other children, or their parents, were cruel to him. But this was different, deeper. Since then, Striker found he often had to find a place alone to vent the emotions that threatened to crush him. It was as if Micah's kindness and Willow's rejection had pierced his very heart.

The sound of the steps grew nearer and Striker wiped at this eyes. A few minutes later a shadow fell across him.

"Hello, may I have a minute of your time?" The voice was deep and strong.

Striker squinted up at the stranger curiously. The man looked to be as tall as a staff. His clothes were brown and forest green, clean but not showy like those of the castle visitors or the merchants Striker had chanced to see. The stranger stood alert and aware of his surroundings. Striker wondered if perhaps the man was a castle guard. He would catch it from Uncle Harron if his protector found out he had spoken to a guard from the castle. He was never to go anywhere near the castle or he would be restrained. Striker unconsciously adjusted his leather wrist guards. At the moment, he did not care about any of that. Uncle Harron was dutiful and firm. He did not actually care for Striker, he only cared that his charge feared and obeyed him. Sometimes it almost seemed like Uncle Harron was the one who carried the curse instead of Striker.

The stranger cleared his throat, drawing Striker's mind back to the present.

Striker looked up at the stranger boldly. "What do you want?" He had no fear, for he had never met anyone who dared to harm him.

"I would like to talk to you," The stranger answered politely. He made no move to intrude without invitation.

Sitting up, Striker jerked a long stalk of wild grass from the dirt. He played it through his fingers, watching the stranger. "You were already talking to me." he finally pointed out.

A smile creased the man's eyes and the boy was drawn to him. "Very perceptive. Would you mind if I join you here and we talk some more?"

"No one ever asks me if I mind things." Striker eyed him warily. "Do you know who I am?"

A shadow of sadness passed over the man's kind face. "I know who you are. And I also know who they say you are."

It was Striker's turn to frown. "What do you mean by that?"

"May I join you?"

"I do not care if you want to sit here. I do not own this field."

Crouching down so he was at eye level with Striker, the man spoke gently. "You asked me what I meant. And so I will tell you. They say you are a curse, a menace, a burden."

Striker's teeth clenched. He started to rise but the man's next words stopped him.

"But they are wrong. They do not know who you really are."

Lowering himself back to the grass where he had been sitting, Striker waited.

"I cannot tell you the whole story. The time is not yet right. But I want you to know that I am here for you."

"Just suddenly showed up after 14 years?" Striker did not hide the accusation in his tone.

Again the stranger's expression was sad. "No, I have been here, but you could not know it yet."

Striker's eyes narrowed. "Thanks, but no thanks." He rose and tossed the grass aside.

"You do not have to be what they tell you that you are." The stranger had also stood.

"What if that is what I am?" Striker demanded. They were nearly the same height and Striker met the man's sad, serious expression with a skeptical glare. "For fourteen years I have carried the curse of Choi. Fourteen years of this wretched dye and the hateful looks it brings. Fourteen years of being restrained like an animal if I cross Uncle Harron or to keep me from being a part of the town's celebrations. Now you show up with your cryptic sayings and tell me that you have been hanging around watching me all these years. Why have you done nothing to help me? Why should I believe I am not what they say? It is all I know, and all I will ever be." Striker strode angrily through the tall grass away from the stranger.

"The day at the pool when you could not swim, how did you get out?" the stranger called after him.

Striker paused but did not turn to face him.

"The leather wrist guards that you wear to protect you

from pain, where did they come from? The day you walked too far and could not find water, where did the canteen and food by the road come from?"

Tears slid down Striker's face, but still he did not face the stranger.

"You are so much more than they say you are. They say you bring pain, but I saw you caring for the Widow Zina when her back was hurt. You brought her so much joy those last few years." He was coming toward Striker, the boy could tell by the nearness of his voice. "They say you bring a curse, but I saw you last year when you saved little Eber from the swimming pool when all the others ran for help. They say you are a burden, but I know that you have brought the town of Choi more goodness than they could ever know."

The man's hand rested lightly on Striker's shoulder. Striker spun, freeing himself. No one ever touched him unless they sought to restrain him. He was prepared to run when the stranger slowly sank to one knee before him.

"Do not let their fear and lack of knowledge drive you to become what they say you are." A tear ran down the stranger's sun-browned face. "How I wish I could take you now. But you must endure a little while longer. The legend of the curse is meant to protect you. It is poorly done, but you cannot allow it to swallow you up. You must trust that I will come back for you when the time is right."

"Why did you come now, after so many years?" Striker asked, wiping the tears from his own face.

"The time is near. You are no longer a child. I can trust you now to say nothing of our meeting." He rose and slipped his hand into the small pouch that hung by a strap across his chest. "I feared you could not endure much longer without a hint of the truth." When he removed his hand, there was a small, well carved wooden hawk in his fingers.

The stranger reached out and took Striker's ugly purple

hand with his left hand and turned it palm up. Placing the wooden bird on the boy's palm, his kind eyes met Striker's. "Rise above what they say," the stranger's eyes were gentle. "You are not what they say you are."

He closed his big hand over Striker's, causing Striker's fingers to close around the piece of wood. "I will come back for you."

CHAPTER 8

"Striker, you know this ridiculous game is futile." Uncle Harron's voice was not quite a shout, but as close as he could come to one without losing his dignity. He stood at the head of a crowd of men. They were there to re-dye and restrain him in preparation for the grand ball the following evening. It happened every year, the dipping of his right hand and left side of his face into the warm tub of purple dye. Uncle Harron said it was to protect the town. If someone did not recognize the Striker, he could endanger the whole village with one careless act.

Every year they hunted Striker like an animal to hold him down and mark him as a menace. Every year he was restrained in a large iron cage for one night. This was to keep him from setting foot on the castle grounds which would bring a year of curses upon the fearful townspeople of Choi.

Some years Striker yielded to them putting up only a half-hearted flight. Last year, he had given them a run for their money and found it to be quite sporting. This time, however, he was not balking them for the sport of it. He would be sixteen years old this year, and he was tired of the whole system. For fifteen years he had lived as a curse, knowing the townspeople were kind only because they were afraid. Fifteen years of living off the charity of people who wished he did not exist had put a bad taste in his mouth. Now, instead of running, he was carelessly sitting up in a tree just within the Forbidden Forest. A crowd of farmers and townspeople had gathered for the day of sport, but they were obviously tiring of the wait. Dinner would be getting cold, and they were ready to have it over with. All their pleas and bargains had done nothing to move the lanky teen who glared defiantly back at them from the tree.

"I'll go deeper into the forest if you do not leave me alone," Striker threatened loudly. "Then a wild animal might find me and maul me to pieces. Think what would happen to your sweet, little town if that happened." He noticed several men exchanged hopeful glances. They were wondering if an animal could kill the Striker without bringing harm on their families.

"Come now, Striker. Be reasonable. It is only one night." Uncle Harron was getting desperate. The sun was sliding downward and they did not have much time to mark and restrain the Striker before the sun set.

"I do not enjoy being dipped like a piece of laundry." Striker replied firmly. "Nor do I enjoy being chained like a mad dog."

"If you had not broken out of the cage four years ago we would not have to use the chains." The farmer was irritated and was having trouble restraining himself. They had been pursuing Striker for three days now and were not any closer to their goal than when they started.

"A cage is not much better in case you have not had the pleasure of the experience." Striker shot back. "I did not come to your castle party or bring any curses on your head, did I? No, I just went home and to bed like a normal boy. There is very little that is normal that I can enjoy. I have no desire to go to your ball. I just want to be left alone."

"Let us mark you and we will discuss it further," Uncle Harron suggested.

Striker laughed. "That worked when I was five and again

when I was seven, dear uncle, but it will not work again. Your further discussions always end up with me in chains."

The men were murmuring together, and Striker did not like the looks they were giving him from behind Uncle Harron. Pretending not to notice, Striker rubbed his chin thoughtfully with his pale purple hand. "But perhaps you are right, Uncle." Moving carefully, Striker slid easily from his perch and made a show of dusting himself off. The men were eager to have him. Some ventured a little nearer to the Forbidden Forest to be the first to get their hands on him once the curse-bearer emerged from the knee high foliage.

"Striker, please." Uncle Harron saw through the act. Anticipating the lean young man's flight into the forest, he moved forward slightly. "It is for your own good."

Striker paused. His uncle had said that before. He always said it softly, as if he meant it more than anything else he said. The older man's eyes were pleading. "They will not have the new year's celebration if you are not bound."

Striker's resolve wavered. Though he feared Uncle Harron more than anything else, the wise man was the only one who stood between Striker and the unstable inhabitants of Choi. Though he feigned bravery, the legends of the Forbidden Forest's dangers kept Striker from actually entering beyond the first line of trees. With a heavy sigh, Striker stepped from the knee high grasses and into their rough, eager grasp. Another year of bondage and yet the man with the kind promises and deep voice had not appeared.

Striker sat crouched against the wall of their cottage. On a torn scrap of paper he was carefully making marks with a makeshift reed pen. Uncle Harron had proper pens, and clean paper, but Striker knew if he asked, the older man would want to know what he was writing. Looking over the marks and drawings that littered the uneven surface of the paper, Striker sighed. What if it were true? What if he was not a curse like everyone said. Could the stranger be right? A year had passed since he had spoken to Striker. Now, Striker was newly dyed and the celebration had proceeded without event. Supposedly that meant it would be a good year. A wry smile crossed his face. He had certainly given them a run for their money this year before he had allowed himself to be caged.

Striker laid the paper on a piece of old leather and folded them both carefully together. Placing it into a divot in the dirt, he replaced the small but heavy floor stone to conceal it. Carefully smoothing the dust around the stone to hide any cracks, Striker stood and surveyed his work. Tossing his old threadbare shirt from last year on top of the place, he carefully wiped his hands on his pants and turned toward the door.

There stood Uncle Harron, his brows furrowed in anger.

Striker could feel the color draining from his face. A cold tingly feeling rushed through him.

"Dig it up again." Uncle Harron commanded fiercely.

"It's nothing, Uncle Harron."

Uncle Harron stepped toward Striker and the young man cowered away as if he had been struck. Slinking to the place, Striker worked his fingers into the hidden crack. Behind him, Striker heard Uncle Harron pulling out the dreaded chains from their box.

Striker spun to face his protector.

"Why are you getting those? I am obeying you." Though he did not realize it, Striker now stood a full head above Uncle Harron. The purple dye on his face made him seem almost ghostly in the flickering firelight. Uncle Harron stopped, his hand still grasping the chains. He studied the boy before him. Striker's face was pleading. The hurt he felt was evident in the angry tears that had sprung up. Uncle Harron knew that the wrong response from him could break in an instant the hold he had on Striker.

"Perhaps I acted hastily," he said gently. "Follow my instructions and there will be no need for these." Turning from Striker, Uncle Harron broke the intensity of the moment. He took his time putting the chains away, giving Striker time to cool off. It worked. Uncle Harron heard Striker's breathing slow. Moving to his bookshelf, Uncle Harron browsed the titles and picked one for that evening's study. Behind him, he heard quiet scraping as Striker uncovered the stone and pulled it from the floor. A slight rustle met his keen ears and the old man turned casually to lay the book on the table.

Striker stood undecided with a crumpled paper in his hands.

"There have never been any secrets between us, Striker. It would be such a shame to have one now." He sat on the wooden chair which creaked loudly in the tense silence. "We will have to repair this chair again. It is no longer content to play the role it was designed to have."

Striker's head cocked slightly as if a new thought had struck him.

"You may place it here on the table." Uncle Harron let a hint of command into his tone.

It worked. As if by habit, Striker walked slowly to the table and laid the dirty paper before Uncle Harron.

Since Uncle Harron had discovered and burned Striker's hideout at the Widow Zina's, Striker no longer had anything of his own besides the dirty mat, the clothes he wore, and the little chair in the corner. Even those items were not actually his. He thought of the wooden hawk and smothered the tiny smile it brought. That was hidden well and would not be discovered.

Uncle Harron finished finding his place in the book before looking up at the paper. He glanced up at Striker. "You should have asked me for paper." It was in his hand now and Striker was once more in his power. "What is this?"

Striker shrugged, "I was practicing my writing."

Uncle Harron frowned slightly as he looked over the odd scratches that covered the paper. There were tally marks and rude sketches of things he could not make out. Fury boiled up inside him. "What is this?" he demanded with an eerie calm.

"Micah's father was injured after I visited their farm." Striker did not meet the older man's eye. "I wanted to tell him I was sorry."

A short, scornful laugh escaped Uncle Harron. "With this?" He threw it down on the table in disgust. "And you think he would know what it meant?"

Striker shifted uneasily. It was he who was guiding the conversation now. He would not divulge the true meaning of that paper even if it cost him a month in chains. Uncle Harron could keep the paper. It was no longer useful to him. Striker had tracked almost a full year of curses and he knew he was not to blame for all the things that happened in Choi. He had not seen the stranger again, but his message rang clearly in Striker's ears even now.

"Rise above what they say. You are not what they say you are."

"That chicken scratch will only show them how terribly uneducated you are." Uncle Harron shook his head. "I would burn it if I were you."

"Would you teach me to write?" Striker had asked many times over the years. This time was no different. The answer was always the same. What Uncle Harron did not know, was that the Widow Zina had shown him how to form many of the letters before her death. Striker did not dare to practice them, but he knew them in his head and carefully shaped them behind closed eyes at night. "Could I not learn the simplest of words?" Striker asked innocently.

"You have no reason to write anything. I have told you often that I will write for you if the need arises." Uncle Harron looked at him coldly. "And I do not foresee it arising."

Striker nodded and took the paper from the table.

"Burn it." It was not a request.

Striker walked slowly to the fire, solidifying in his memory the patterns and tally marks the paper held. Perhaps he would create it again someday. Until then, it would be safe in his memory.

Striker tossed it into the fire and watched it crumple into black ash. "It is a curse to be so empty headed," Striker muttered loud enough to be overheard. Going to his mat, he lay with his back to the fire and Uncle Harron. Pillowing his head on his hand, Striker closed his eyes and traced the forbidden letters in his mind.

"You think that he knows the truth?" Laden asked unhitching his horse from the plow.

Uncle Harron scowled. "I do not know, Laden. He is changing, hiding something. We may have to act sooner than we planned."

"He is 16 now, Uncle Harron. It is better to move before he is of age, as he will need a counselor to rule in his place," Laden continued casually with his work as they spoke. "If you wait until he is 18, you may not have the position you have suffered so long to secure."

"Do you not think that I have considered this already?" Uncle Harron spat back. He calmed himself and moved in closer to Laden. "I will go and see the king. Perhaps things can be moved forward at a faster rate."

"I will leave it to you then." Laden patted the horse's neck and led him into the barn.

CHAPTER 9

Whistling was expressly forbidden. Uncle Harron said it would bring terrible consequences on the town if the bearer of the curse were to whistle a tune in the town. This is why Striker found himself alone beside the highway. There he could whistle all the cheery tunes he desired out of sight and hearing of the town of Choi. He was wise enough now to know the only reason his whistling was deemed a curse was because it annoyed Uncle Harron.

Striker was quite good at whistling now, having had many hours alone beside the deserted highway to practice. He could hit almost any note he wanted. The highway went over a rise which allowed Striker to see a good distance in every direction. No one could approach and be whistled upon without Striker's knowledge. And thus, no one would be hurt by the curse of the Striker's merry whistle. More importantly, no one would bring news of it back to Uncle Harron.

Striker's lips were tired. He had come mid-morning and had whistled every tune that came to mind. Now, the sun was fully up and the heat of it warmed the land. Laying in the damp grass, Striker closed his eyes and let the sun's warmth seep into him.

"Ho there!"

Striker jerked awake and scrambled to his feet. Two men stood in the road looking at him expectantly.

"What luck is this?" one of the men crowed, gesturing

toward Striker. "See his funny painted face, Clance? This is none other than the court jester. We are on the right road at last." Turning his attention to the stunned young man, the stranger went on, "Tell me good sir, where is your master's castle. We have business there."

Striker's eyes grew wide and fearful. He was forbidden to be by the highway, he was forbidden to whistle, he was forbidden to speak to strangers, he had probably disobeyed a thousand other commands, but his mind was too dazed to remember what they were. "Speak up, man, I have asked you a question."

"Perhaps he is mute, Troy." the bold man's companion offered.

Striker glanced at the man, pursing his lips together into a hard line. Yes, he would be mute. Even if he had not known every person in Choi, the clothes of the men would have given them away as foreigners. They were not fancy and impractical, but the cloth was of fine soft weave and the colors were bright and pleasant. They reminded Striker of the man who had given him the hawk and the promise, and yet the style was not quite the same. The bold one Striker had heard called Troy was deeply tanned with a close, well cut beard. Clance was only slightly fairer and clean shaven. He had thick black hair that did not seem to settle in any particular direction. It was obvious that both had been traveling for some time.

"Clance, he is clearly not mute," Troy protested. "You do not have to press your lips together to be mute," the bold one pointed out.

Clance shrugged, "He is not doing it now."

"All that tells us is that he speaks our language, or at least understands it. You do understand what we are saying, do you not?"

Striker's eyes darted from one to the other. The stiff fear

had not left him. How would he get away from them? If Uncle Harron… A movement on the road caught Striker's eye. Despair crushed the faint flickering hope Striker had for escape. There, on the road, and hurrying toward them, was Uncle Harron himself.

"What are you doing here?" the old man demanded, breathing heavily from the exertion of climbing the steep hill.

No one could tell who he was addressing, so they all stood gaping at the old man.

Troy nudged his companion and gave a slight nod toward the boy.

Striker's face, the side that was not dyed purple, had gone white, and he looked as if a gust of wind would knock him from his feet. He was trembling, and the fingers of his purple hand toyed nervously with the leather guard on his left wrist.

"Ho now, good sir. It seems you have put some kind of fear into the youth." He stepped forward and offered Uncle Harron his hand. "I am Troy, and this is my traveling companion, Clance. We are here to see your king."

"Strangers are not welcome here in Choi. You come unannounced and will not be welcomed into the castle."

"You certainly know a lot about the castle," Troy observed coolly. "Perhaps you can give us directions. This lad seems to be somewhat tongue tied at present."

Troy was rewarded by a grateful glance from the boy and a glare from the newcomer.

"You are not welcome here," Uncle Harron repeated.

Troy moved closer to him. "I do not believe the introductions were completed. We did not get your name, or the name of the boy here."

"I am Uncle Harron, counselor of the king. The boy is of no consequence."

The men did not miss the threatening look Uncle Harron gave Striker or the shrinking fear that the look produced in the strange young man.

"At last, someone who will be able to give us guidance. I can see you are a learned man. And such a title as Uncle tells me that you are very well respected in this area. We are honored to have happened upon you. The boy was of no use at all." Putting his hand on one side of his mouth, Troy added confidentially, "I fear he is not all there in the head. We could not get a word out of him."

Again the look of relief passed over the old man's face. This was what he wanted to hear. The flattery was effective. They saw him relax ever so slightly. A little color crept back into the boy's face.

"You see," Troy leaned casually against the large marker rock beside the highway, "we have heard so much about your town that we could not bear not to come. The legend of the Striker has leaked out over the years, and we wanted very much to see the young man for ourselves. How you kept it a secret for so long is beyond my comprehension. The boy must be at least sixteen years old by now, if my calculations are correct. We came to visit the king and to see a legend. Instead, all we find is this painted youth, who is a very poor jester from what we can tell. Half the fun of a royal jester is his witty tongue. This boy has no wit at all."

"So you came to make a show of the curse our town must bear?" Uncle Harron demanded.

"No, of course not," Clance corrected quickly. "We were sent to pay our respects to the old king as news has come that he is not well."

Troy leaned in confidingly and added, "But I must admit that the Striker has peaked our interest. In all the surrounding countries, a 'striker' is someone who looks exceptionally like another person. So much so that the two could be twins, or at the least, very closely related."

Striker's mind reeled. He had forced Mort to tell him

the story so often that one line shot through his mind like an arrow. "She looked fearfully at a picture of the crowned prince on the wall…and then into Uncle Harron's eyes… 'He's a Striker!'" A striker was a look alike, not a curse. That was why his face was marred with dark dye. Uncle Harron was doing his best to hide the resemblance. Could it be that Striker looked that much like Prince Deetry, even at birth? Emmery was best midwife in Choi. Striker had often heard the farmer's wives blaming him for her disappearance. If she was the best, was it not possible that she had also assisted the queen when Prince Deetry was born?

Uncle Harron had seen the change in Striker. Grabbing the teen's limp wrist, he tugged him along toward the safety of Choi. There he could alert the farmers of the danger. They would be able to stop these men and send them away before more harm was done. He had planned too long to have it all crumble to pieces in one day. The old king was ailing and was almost convinced to leave the kingdom to Harron instead of his obstinate son who had disobeyed him so publically 17 years before. Harron had worked hard to keep that rift between the royals fresh over the years. If the king refused, Harron had the king's grandson as a bargaining chip that could not fail. Striker was the link between two kingdoms. If a grandson existed, King Deetrin must admit and abide by the treaty formed by his rebellious son's marriage. He would not want the boy, and for a handsome title would be willing to make an exchange to ensure the boy never claimed his throne. Laden was right, perhaps he had waited too long. Preoccupied with his thoughts, Uncle Harron tugged the stumbling young man as he hurried back toward Choi.

Falling in behind them and matching the old man's brisk pace, Troy noticed the dazed boy did not resist the older man's grasp or guidance. He saw the leather on the young man's free wrist bore deep lines—lines that would be caused by the chafing of metal closed tightly around it. Troy glanced at Clance and knew by his slight nod that his traveling companion had noticed the marks as well. This young man was the Striker they sought.

They strode after the flustered uncle and caught up easily with the pair. Striker's mind raced as he stumbled along beside the older man almost oblivious of Uncle Harron's tight hold on his wrist.

"Choi is such a little town to have so many legends," Troy observed from where they walked just a pace and a half behind Uncle Harron and his prisoner. "Take the Prince's wife for instance."

Uncle Harron's pace increased, but the strangers were tall and kept up easily with the old man's short stride. Striker stumbled and fell to one knee, catching himself with his purple right hand. Righting himself, Striker glanced back at them, begging them silently to go on. A jerk from Uncle Harron brought Striker's attention back to the road ahead.

"It looks like we might have a bit of a walk ahead, Troy. Tell me the legend again. It has been some time since I have heard it all."

"Silence you fools!" Uncle Harron turned on them sharply, but he held no power over the strangers. They only blinked at him in surprise. When he turned away and began hurrying toward town once more, they continued casually with their previous conversation.

"She came to Choi in a carriage from a far away land," Troy began.

"Oreathia, was it not?"

"Ah, yes, the fair land of Oreathia," Troy agreed. "Her hair was as wavy as the sea and as dark as the raven's wing. As a matter of fact, her hair color was identical to that of this silent lad traveling with us." Troy ignored the cold glare the uncle sent his way. His uneasiness only proved their suspicions were right. This old man knew exactly who the boy was.

"Go on," Clance prompted when Troy's thoughtful silence grew too long.

"She was such a beauty that farmers for miles would stop their work to catch a glimpse of her as her carriage passed by on the way to the castle. Rumor had it that she was to be wed to Prince Deetry, despite the king's public forbidding of the union. The rumor proved true when Prince Deetry announced that he and the beauty had been secretly married for three days. This, as you will remember, is the time required after the marriage before a new wife becomes an heir to her husband's estate. The old king was furious. How he raged! And you would not have believed the terrible threats the servants heard him breathe. He tried desperately to persuade his son to silently put her away. Prince Deetry, however, loved the beauty and would not waver in his commitment to her. The king made plans to send her far away into exile but someone alerted her before they could be carried out. That very night, she fled the castle. Brokenhearted and knowing the risks, the young lady fled into the Forbidden Forest. There she was lost. Search parties could find no trace of her, and as the months passed, even Prince Deetry gave up hope. The whole town knew that she had been taken by the evils of the Forbidden Forest."

Uncle Harron was almost jogging now. They were nearing Laden's farm. He knew he could trust Laden to take Striker away and hide him until this blew over.

The strangers jogged along easily behind them, always keeping pace with Uncle Harron.

"If I remember right," Clance observed, "the forest was not forbidden until after the Striker was born."

"Your memory serves you well, Clance. When the beauty could not be found, the forest was forbidden. The people saw to it that the unknown was soon filled with legends of terrors that lurked inside to keep their children from venturing inside. They say the king even dug deep pits to make the forest more treacherous. One night," Troy went on, "not quite a year later, a worn, sickly woman emerged from the forest. She was great with child and near to death from starvation. Some entertained notions that she was the same beauty that was lost, but the fantasy did not last. No one could have survived in the Forbidden Forest for so long. Legends say that many mighty warriors have tried to tame the evils of the forest and are never seen again."

"Do you think they are true?" Clance asked casually.

Troy shrugged, then said for the sake of Striker, "There's only one way to find out, I suppose. Anyway, the sickly woman was nearly out of her mind. Her face bore witness of the horrors she had seen in the forest. It seemed that the poor creature had even lost the ability to speak. There was not even a hint of beauty about her."

Uncle Harron swerved off the main highway, dragging Striker along with him down a rutted trail through the tall grass. "Laden! Come quickly we are in grave danger!" he shouted.

"She gave birth to a child." Troy's story continued defiantly before the man's shout had died away. "Rumor has it that the midwife who was at the delivery declared the child to be a striker—A person almost identical in looks to someone she had seen before. It was a much younger Emmery who delivered the prince twenty-seven years before this child was born. But she remembered the day vividly. After all, Choian royalty share the same distinct features. And so, when Emmery saw him, she knew this child was..."

"Laden?!" Uncle Harron's voice had risen to a desperate scream.

"He is not at home today." All four jerked to a halt at the sound of the boy's soft voice.

"He is not mute after all." Clance observed.

"Where is he?" Uncle Harron demanded, roughly jerking Striker forward again.

"He is at the blacksmith's on the other side of town. His bay threw a shoe yesterday."

Uncle Harron's jaw muscles worked and he clenched his teeth in anger. Suddenly a strange calm came over him and he turned to the strangers. His voice was too polite. It seemed unnatural after his desperate shouts for help a moment before.

"I see you know the rumors very well. You will come to my house for tea and we will discuss this further. After we have spoken, if you are still determined to see the king, I will take you to him myself."

The strangers looked at one another. Troy shrugged and Clance nodded their consent.

"You must say no more until we reach my home," Uncle Harron instructed.

They did not object to the terms. What needed to be said had been said already.

Willie was the first person they encountered on their way to Uncle Harron's house. He ran off quickly after a word from Uncle Harron. He was to find Laden and bring him as quickly as possible. The boy made good time, and people were lining up to gawk at the newcomers before they had entered the official town square. Turning left at the dry fountain, the little party made its way to the house shared by Striker and Uncle Harron.

Laden rode up on a borrowed horse as they approached the door.

"Take the boy and keep him safe. I wish to have tea with these men and find out more about their purpose in coming to Choi."

Laden clearly understood more than what was said.

He dismounted and warily approached Striker. Taking the young man's free wrist, he nodded to show he had a firm grip. Uncle Harron released Striker's other arm. Laden tugged and Striker followed without thinking. It was how it always happened. Fighting them had never bought him freedom once they had him by the wrist.

"Wait. Taking the boy was not part of the agreement." Troy protested.

"He'll be safe. Come, we will refresh ourselves. I will make a fresh pot of tea."

Striker jerked to a stop. Tea. In a flash he remembered the image of Widow Zina sprawled on her kitchen floor. On the table there had been a partially drunk cup of tea. In all his visits, Striker had never seen the widow make tea. The little girl who had died last summer, there had been no mark on her, and Striker was blamed for her death. Mort's tabby and little Eber's puppy had all met the same fate. He had been told that it was his affection that brought their deaths.

"Come on, we will get you settled." Laden pulled and Striker moved forward.

Suddenly it all clicked in Striker's mind. He pulled against Laden's grasp, desperately locking eyes with the strangers. "Do not drink the..."

Laden clapped a hand over Striker's mouth, stifling his words. Striker, in desperation, bit the big man's finger hard. Gasping, Laden jerked his hand away.

"The tea!" Striker shouted frantically, "Do not drink..."

This time, Laden's big hand clamped on Strikers face. His palm on one side of his jaw and finger tips on the other keeping the middle of his hand a safe distance from the young man's teeth. This pulled Striker's cheeks inward so that if he did try to bite, he would bite the inside of his cheeks before getting anywhere near Laden's fingers.

Striker shouted another warning but his words were

muffled by his captor's hand and could not be understood.

With his left arm around Striker, grasping his right wrist, and his other covering the boy's mouth, Laden started walking, calmly dragging Striker with him. Laden was burly and strong. Pull and twist as he might, Striker could not free himself.

Troy opened his mouth to protest, but Uncle Harron dismissed his concern with a wave of his hand. "He is our Striker, gentlemen, the bearer of our town's curse. No one will hurt him. You must not mind his tantrums. He often reacts that way when he does not get his way. Laden will calm him, and he will not be hurt."

CHAPTER 10

Striker struggled against Laden until he was out of sight of the visitors. Once Laden felt him give in, the big farmer took Striker by the wrist, and they traveled quickly across the square and behind the Town Hall. In minutes, he was shoved roughly into the metal cage. His right wrist was encircled with the iron cuff that was soldered to the bars. Although he knew it was hopeless, Striker fought Laden as the man tried to get the second cuff around his other wrist. Writhing and twisting in the small space, Striker was talking fast.

"Laden, he's going to kill the king and Prince Deetry. Let me go, listen to me. Uncle Harron is the curse of Choi. He is the one responsible for the deaths and accidents, not me. He killed Widow Zina and the little Foster girl. He did it with the tea. Please Laden, listen to me. I am not the curse. We have to protect the king. We have to protect my father."

Laden froze, holding Striker's free wrist in one hand and the cuff in the other, just inches apart.

"Your father? Are you mad? How dare you claim to be related to Prince Deetry! You, who were born a curse. You, who has brought only death and suffering to Choi."

"I did not know it until today, Laden. Listen to me, please. Uncle Harron is going to kill the king and the prince. They trust him. He is going to kill them and try to use me to take the throne for himself."

An evil gleam came into Laden's eyes. "Then we had

better keep you safe where you can be found." With a quick movement, Laden clicked the cuff in place around Striker's wrist.

————————

Inside Uncle Harron's house, Troy and Clance stood waiting as the respected scholar prepared the promised tea. Clance gestured with his chin toward the pitiful mat in the far corner of the room. The dogs of noble men had better places to sleep than the Striker of Choi. A frown crossed Troy's face. They both saw the iron ring fastened to the thick support beam and the scarred wood around it.

"Do you have a pet?" Troy asked, gesturing toward the matt and ring.

"Oh, that," Uncle Harron searched for words. There were very few besides Striker who dared to enter his home, so he had not considered how it could look to a stranger. "In a way."

"How can you have a dog in a way? Either you have a dog, or you do not have a dog," Troy responded in irritation.

"Or perhaps it is not a dog but you treat him as one," Clance suggested softly.

Uncle Harron shrugged. "My property is my concern, gentlemen, not yours. The tea will be ready any minute. Please, be seated." He regretted his words as soon as they were spoken. There were only two chairs in the room. One of the chairs, a fine well sanded piece, sat neat and inviting by the table. The other, a crooked stool without a back, sat crammed in the corner as if its owner preferred to cower there, far from the owner of the first chair.

"I suppose that is your partial dog's chair?" Troy asked, pointing at it over his shoulder with his thumb.

"The tea is almost ready." Uncle Harron was willing it to boil, but the water simply wavered peacefully in the little pot.

Troy's eyes darted toward the open door when the old man's back was turned. Clance gave a quick, short nod of his head to show he understood.

"Tell me, Uncle, how is it that you, a learned man, came to live so long hidden away in the town of Lesser Choi?" Troy asked casually.

"I am close to the castle where a counselor should be," Uncle Harron responded, sparing a glance at the bold stranger. Perhaps more wood was needed. But he did not dare to leave the strangers alone in his house. There was no telling what they would try to search through or find out. No, he must be patient. It would not be long before these men were taken care of.

"Where did you get your learning?" Troy tried again. "So many books line that wall there. You have read them all?"

If Uncle Harron had a weakness, it was his education. He glanced at Troy with an amused smile. "I have read them many times over. And more besides those that were loaned to me from nobility."

Troy shook his head and whistled in awe. "You must be the wisest man living."

Uncle Harron chuckled self-consciously. "Not the wisest, but I like to think I am close to it." He glanced over to see what the quiet stranger thought of his reputation. Clance was no longer in the house. "Where is he?" Uncle Harron demanded. His voice had lost the soft tone of false humility.

Troy responded with a shrug, "He does not care for tea. I think he stepped out for some fresh air."

"Go get him at once!" Uncle Harron demanded. He caught himself, and added, "It is customary for guests to be refreshed at my home and for me to hear their purpose before they come before the king and the prince. To show up uninvited would result in imprisonment."

"That is a fine custom. Does the boy help you prepare

for them?"

Uncle Harron's eyes narrowed. "It seems, sir, that your purpose in coming is not one that will please the king. Displease me and you will not see the king."

"Perhaps not. I will go and find Clance. If we are not welcome here, we will be on our way."

"In a moment," Uncle Harron's tone was chilling.

Troy watched the thin stream of steaming liquid as the old man poured it into a sturdy cup. The thick odor filled the room and Troy found it hard to think.

The old man turned and set the cup on the table near where Troy stood. "First you must have your tea."

"Laden, that is what he called you, am I correct?" Clance strode toward the man with a casual, friendly air.

"What are you doing here?" Laden demanded. He moved between Clance and the cage that held Striker as if to unconsciously block it from the stranger's sight.

Striker was sitting with his knees up against his chest, his wrists were chained to the side of the cage near his right shoulder. "Get away!" Striker shouted desperately. For once he understood what Uncle Harron had been doing. The fear and despair he felt were evident in his tear stained face. "Don't let your friend drink the tea. It will kill him. You have to get him away from Uncle Harron while you can!" Striker begged.

"I came to see the Striker," Clance responded casually, addressing Laden.

"You have seen him. Now move along. Even the Striker is advising it."

"What does he know?" His tone was careless but Clance's eyes were telling another story which Laden did not miss.

"I see you come armed against a common farmer." Laden

pointed out the dagger that was strapped to Clance's side. Striker had not noticed it before.

"Common farmer?" Clance laughed. "And I am a road weary vagabond. So together we should be a fairly even pair."

Striker knew that if Laden had spread rumor that the strangers meant to harm him, the other farmers would be assembling, stealing towards them with any weapon they could get their hands on. The newcomer's dagger would be little help against their number. "They will be coming. Please get away. There are too many of them."

"Silence, Curse!" Laden threatened, keeping his attention on Clance.

"You are not a farmer, sir. And so, finding a man like you here," Clance's gesture enveloped the dusty street and the back of the town hall building that was in much need of a new coat of whitewash, "leads me to only one conclusion. That you are working with Harron."

"Uncle Harron."

"And will you be Uncle Laden when this is over? Or perhaps Lord Laden? That has a bit of a ring to it, does it not?"

"Please, you are wasting time. Uncle Harron will kill your friend." Striker scrambled to his knees, jerking against the cuffs he wore. "You must warn him."

"Perhaps you should not have been so friendly with them on the road, Striker," Laden responded coolly. "Uncle Harron has often warned you about talking to strangers."

Striker ignored Laden completely. "Please go to him. He will need you."

Something in Striker's desperation rang true, and Clance knew at once he should not have left Troy alone with such a dangerous man. According to the boy, the old man had killed before. One more victim would mean very little. Especially if the killing was done so cleanly as with a cup of tea.

Clance backed up to where he could see down the side

of the building, keeping his eyes on Laden. The common farmer was moving and circling coolly like a prize fighter.

Clance caught sight of a farmer who dashed across the open area carrying a pitchfork over his shoulder. He met Striker's eyes over Laden who was crouched and ready to charge. "I will come back," he said to Striker.

With a quick pivot, Clance raced back the way he had come and out of sight around the town hall stable.

Laden straightened and put his thick fists on his hips. This would get him a raise in position when Uncle Harron came to power.

———————

Troy sat as if in a stupor staring into the mug of tea. His hands were in his lap, clenched. There was something about that tea. Something he had to remember. He was no longer aware of the strong, sweet odor of the tea. Somewhere in the background, the old man was droning on. His words gently worked their way into Troy's head. The old man wanted Troy to drink the tea. Why should he not drink it? Troy frowned at the dark, steaming liquid.

Uncle Harron glanced at the open door. This man's mind was much stronger than the others he had given tea. But then, the others had trusted him until it was too late. The king would trust him. Prince Deetry, too, would succumb out of royal etiquette.

The other stranger had gotten away, but somehow Uncle Harron knew this man was the one he needed to worry about. "Just try a little, sir. You will find it soothing and warm," Uncle Harron murmured softly. "It will soothe away your troubles."

Troy could not pull his eyes away from the steaming mug. His hands clenched tighter in his lap as his mind fought the numbing effects of the odor.

A tiny open vile that hung around Harron's neck provided another scent for the older man to breath. It kept his mind clear as he moved slowly, but casually, towards the stranger. "Come now," Uncle Harron spoke gently in a calming tone. "Would you insult an old man by refusing refreshment?" A sound outside caused Uncle Harron to turn sharply towards the door. There was someone coming. There was very little time to take care of the stranger now.

Whether he moved too quickly and triggered an automatic reaction or if the scent of the vile around his neck caused Troy to regain his power of thought, Troy could not say. As Uncle Harron reached for the mug to bring it to the man's lips himself, Troy came to himself in an instant. His clenched hands flew upward to protect his face, knocking the mug out of the old man's hand.

"Away with that bewitching brew!" Troy flung the chair back as he sprang to his feet. There he wavered, unsure. Already the smell was closing in again. He stumbled toward the open door.

Uncle Harron grabbed a blade from the counter and swiftly followed his guest.

CHAPTER 11

Striker writhed against the chains, twisting them tighter and tighter in the hopes that by some miracle they would give way. His wrists ached. If the strangers died, it would be his fault. All the guilt he lived with was placed on him by Uncle Harron. This time, it would be justified. Striker should have known. He should have been able to make sense of the whole charade years ago. The man who gave him the hawk had known. Why had he not helped before now? Why had he hidden the truth? Even as he asked, Striker knew the answer. Had he known he was a prince, Striker would have exposed himself. He would have tried to confide in people, and one by one they would have been killed by Uncle Harron.

All of the anguish and anger burst inside. Throwing back his head, Striker screamed. Again and again he jerked against the chains with all his might. Exhausted, he let his head fall back against the solid back wall of the cage. It was solid because it blocked the view of the castle which, in reality, could not be seen from there even from outside the cage. So many superstitions he had always known and never had the whit to question.

Looking absently at his hands, Striker noticed that his left hand was bruising purple where the cuff had jammed against the base of his hand. Using his purple right hand, Striker tried to squeeze his left hand small enough to go through the cuff. It was too swollen from his previous efforts. Again his head fell back against the solid metal. Then, as he had always done ever since he could remember, Striker stopped struggling. Escaping was hopeless, just as it had always been.

––––––––––

A shadow filled the doorway. Uncle Harron looked up to see Clance, Troy's companion. The older man could not see the stranger's expression, but he could feel the negative emotion and the cold tingle of fear that filled him. The smell would work on this one as well, the tea would have to be shared. There was only one cup of it left in the pan. It would still kill them, but their deaths would take longer than Harron had to wait.

As if sensing Uncle Harron's thoughts, Clance's hand moved to the hilt of his own blade.

"I am so glad you returned. Your friend is not feeling well." Uncle Harron's concerned tone was almost believable.

"And the blade?" Clance asked, nodding toward the knife in the old man's hand.

"I was going to cut some cake to go with the tea." Uncle Harron answered. "When your friend stumbled, I suppose I forgot to put it down when I went to help him. Does he faint often? Come, sit him here in the chair, and I will see if some tea will clear his head."

"You forget, sir that I have traveled for some time with Troy. I will not be taken in by your lies about him."

Uncle Harron could hear the controlled anger in the man's voice.

"Throw down your knife." Clance paused, the strong smell was overwhelming. Stepping outside where the breeze could dissipate the odor, Clance kept his eyes on the old man. "Throw it into the fire."

Uncle Harron hesitated, glancing at Troy who was standing unsteadily in the middle of the room, his mind muddled by the odor.

Something small and hard struck Uncle Harron in the chest. He looked down in time to see his precious vile falling from the chain around his neck toward the hard stone floor. The knife fell from his hand as he made a grab for the vile.

It was safe.

In that moment, Clance had crossed the room, grabbed the knife from the floor, and tossed it into the fire. Turning on him, Clance pried the vile out of the protesting uncle's hand. Uncle Harron fled from the house slamming the door shut behind him. Clance put the vile to his nose. His head cleared instantly. He had to be rid of that poisoning odor before he could help Troy. Going to the stove, Clance grabbed the rag-covered pot handle and removed it from the heat. For the first time, he noticed that the little house had no windows. They had been filled in years ago, hiding the inhabitants from the outside world. Taking the rag from the pot handle, Clance dipped it into the water pail and stuffed it into the stove. The fire struggled to engulf the cloth, filling the room with the foul smoke of dying flames.

Going to Troy's side, Clance held the vile for his companion to breath. Troy shook his head slightly and blinked hard.

"Where is the tea?"

"Thirsty? At a time like this?" Clance clicked his tongue to show his disapproval. "What will your father say?"

Troy spotted the dark stain on the table and floor and knew the old man had not overcome him in his stupor. "Where is the boy?"

"Come, we must hurry, I'm sure that is where the uncle was headed."

Clance opened the door and peered out. He jerked back as a knife embedded itself where his head had been seconds before.

"Who is there?" Clance called, keeping behind the door for cover.

"Uncle Harron told me to keep you inside," an older man shouted back. "So that is what I will do until his return."

"There are no windows." Troy spoke Clance's thought aloud. "We're trapped like rats."

"Striker, Laden tells me you spoke as if you had gone mad while he was here with you. Are you feeling well?"

"Where are the strangers?" Striker pulled against the chains to move closer to the front of the cage.

"They are safe. I left them at the cottage to refresh themselves." Uncle Harron's face betrayed his disappointment, and Striker knew they had somehow managed to escape him.

"Forget about them. They will not stay here in Choi. Tell me what you said to Laden."

Striker tried hard to hide the relief he felt. Slipping back into who he was before he understood Uncle Harron's plan was easy on the outside. "Why do I have to be chained?" Striker moaned. "It is not the New Year, or a feast day, or any day that is any different from another. I hate being chained." He let his voice rise to an almost disrespectful volume.

Uncle Harron would have grabbed him, perhaps struck him had they been alone in their cottage. Striker could see it in the old man's eyes. The few townspeople standing a respectful distance away spared the boy a cuffing. Though they could not hear what was said, they could see everything that went on between Uncle Harron and the hated Striker.

"I will not ask you again. Did you tell Laden you were the son of the prince?"

The laughter that escaped Striker was genuine. "He believed it? I got him at last. That will take him off his high horse. Always pushing me around. He is quite rough with me, you know. Why is it the curse never touches Laden? I even spit in his garden every day for a week when I was nine. Not one of his plants died."

"You were joking with him then?" Uncle Harron seemed almost relieved.

Striker's eyes were merry. "It was a good one, was it not? And he believed it. The wildest tale yet was the one that took him in."

"That was a very disrespectful thing to say. You must never say it again. You will bring a curse on the king if you are claiming such things, even in jest," Uncle Harron admonished. "That is a serious offence and I will not tolerate it."

"Very well, I will not jest with Laden about being a king. How could he be so witless as to believe such a tale?" Striker knew he had to make it believable if he was to throw Uncle Harron off the scent.

"You are not to jest about it to anyone. It is a foul lie and not to be repeated. Do you understand?"

Striker read the threat in his tone and nodded seriously. "If I do not use the jest again, will you let me out? My hand is very sore and going numb."

Uncle Harron moved around to where he could get a better look at Strikers left hand. It was swollen and slightly discolored.

"You should not have fought so hard. I am sure an injury like this will bring something terrible on Choi."

"I hope it falls right on Laden's barn!" Striker stated emphatically.

"Silence." Uncle Harron's tone was hard and threatening. "How often must I tell you not to make light of the terrible curse you carry for Choi?"

"Please let me out, Uncle Harron." Striker moved back against the wall of the cage. "I will go straight home and stay on my mat for the rest of the day. I am terribly tired."

"You have acted very poorly today, Striker. I feel a punishment is due. Do you not agree?"

"Please, Uncle Harron. Let it be my dinner tonight." There was no more fight left in the boy. The strangers were safe, and he had convinced Uncle Harron that Laden's charge was simply a jest. Now his life would go on as usual until the strangers had left town and he could find a way to escape. "My hand aches terribly. The cuff is so tight."

"You should not have fought it." Uncle Harron straightened as if to leave.

"Will you not loosen it? I will not move a muscle until you are done. You have my word."

"Your word?" Uncle Harron laughed cruelly. "Your word is worth nothing to me. You must learn to act with more forethought in the future."

Smoothing his tunic, Uncle Harron turned and strode away from the curse of Choi.

CHAPTER 12

"I would not open that door again, if I were you." Mort shouted as Clance eased open the cottage door. A knife came from the direction of the speaker and lodged into the frame, keeping the door from opening. "Uncle Harron has given us strict orders to keep you inside, so you can make yourself comfortable until he returns. So you might as well stop trying to slip out of there. And tell your friend to stop digging through the wall. It is not as if we are deaf."

"But it is Harron who made up the curse." Troy called, trying to buy Clance time. "Can you not see it?"

"Uncle Harron. You will address him properly or that will be the end of our discussion."

Troy shook his head at Clance in disbelief before calling out, "I did not mean to disrespect the wise uncle. I am new to these parts and forgot myself for a moment. Uncle Harron has told you everything about the Striker then?"

"Of course. We have not suffered under the curse of the Striker for so long without learning what happens if he's taken from our town."

"Have you ever considered that Uncle Harron made up the whole tale?"

A hard silence met his accusation.

Clance stopped chipping at the wall and urged Troy to continue. He was almost through the wall. Two exits would double their chance of getting by the sentry.

"A Striker is someone who looks like someone else. Surely you are old enough to remember that." Troy called. "And who does the boy look like, sir? If you really think about it, who does he resemble?"

Again, there was silence.

"He is Prince Deetry's son by the forbidden marriage." Troy said in answer to his own question. "He is a striker only because he looks exactly like his father. We have come to help him and to free Lesser Choi. You must let us out at once."

Mort's response was long in coming. "I am in this too deep to turn back now. The way I treated the boy would land me in the dungeon for life. I was a fool not to see it before, but I have no choice but to stand by Uncle Harron and hope he is merciful."

"And if the young prince were merciful? If you saved his life, would he not pardon you?"

Clance gave him a nod. He had broken through the wall. With a hard shove, the outer wall crumbled away, leaving a gaping hole a man could easily crawl through. Sunlight filled the dim room, illuminating the clouds of dust Clance had stirred up. Troy flattened himself against the inside wall and waited. Nothing.

Clance brought a blanket and moved it before the hole. There was no response from outside. With a quick dive, he was through the hole into the open.

Troy moved the front door and was rewarded with a firm warning from outside. Diving through the hole, Troy rolled to a crouch and grinned over at Clance.

"On to find the young prince."

———————

A slight noise woke Striker from his fitful sleep. The sun still shone, though not quite as brightly as he remembered it being before. His left hand felt as thick as a sausage in the butcher's window display. Without moving, Striker tried to place what had woken him. There was no noise, and Striker opened his eyes slowly. His head ached and his mouth was painfully dry.

He shifted, still supporting his left elbow with his knee in an attempt to relieve some of the pressure of the cuff, and looked around. Still, he saw no one. Yet the sense that someone was close had not left him.

After leaving Striker, Uncle Harron and Laden had held a hushed conference together with frequent glances in Striker's direction. Both looked uncommonly unsettled. They had appointed Ike, the blacksmith, to stand guard before they hurried away in opposite directions.

Striker moved his head to get a clearer view of Ike through the bars. "Ike?" he shouted loudly, knowing the man was nearly deaf.

Ike rose and came nearer. "What is it?"

"My left cuff is very tight."

"I don't have the key." He turned to go, but Striker called him back. "What now?" he asked gruffly. Striker had always loved the thick man's gruff manners and gentle mannerisms.

"Could you cut it off?"

"What was that?"

Striker raised his voice "Could you cut it off?"

"I would do as well to cut off my head if Uncle Harron found out."

"Well?"

Ike laughed his booming laugh. "I'm sorry it's causing you pain, Striker, but you know I cannot remove the cuff. I have a family to think about."

Striker nodded. Ike's children were not unkind like the others, and he did not wish to bring pain upon his family. "Thank you."

Ike wavered, his gentle eyes resting on Striker. "Perhaps I could loosen it if I was very careful with my tools and did not scratch the lock. Your hand does not look good, and such an injury must bring with it something terrible to those involved."

"Would you try?" Striker begged. "I'll be as still as I can."

Ike looked amused. When he was a boy, Striker had often used such promises to escape his captors. Ike's head cocked slightly as he studied Striker through the bars. For the first time, Ike did not see Striker as a child. Instead, he saw a desperate young man pleading for help. "I will try. But you must keep a look out for me."

Striker nodded.

Ike glanced around before giving what he must have thought to be a soft whistle. The sound carried far, and presently, Ike's little, brown dog appeared. Wagging and grinning, it sat at Ike's feet. Ike crouched beside the dog, looked into its bright eyes and said loudly, "Fetch Hans."

The dog yapped once before running off in the direction of the blacksmith's shop.

"He will fetch no one else. Only Hans. The silly dog knows all of my other children, but it is only Hans that he will bring."

Striker glanced nervously around, his eyes always returning to the place where the dog had disappeared. It was not long before the dog appeared followed by the breathless Hans. Ike's oldest boy was not much younger than Striker. He had never been unkind like the other boys, but like the others, Hans avoided Striker as much as possible.

"Mama said to ask if you want me to bring your lunch. The food is nearly ready." Hans spoke close to his father's ear, so he would not have to shout.

"I called you, Hans, for a reason." Ike told him firmly.

Hans ducked his head submissively, very aware of Striker's

curious gaze on him.

"What is it, Pa?"

"I want my tools. Striker's cuff is too tight, and it will injure the town to leave it so."

"But Pa, what will Uncle Harron say?

"Am I the slave of Uncle Harron?" Ike boomed in irritation. "Your father has sent you for something. It is not the time to question or advise."

With a brief glare at Striker, Hans trotted off with the brown dog at his heels.

"What do you want?" Ike's tone had changed, and he drew the long sword he wore as the two strangers approached.

"We are here to let the boy free." Troy spoke honestly, liking the kind face of the blacksmith.

"You cannot. I was set here to guard him. Uncle Harron is not a man to be crossed," Ike warned. He held the sword awkwardly with the point hanging down toward the ground. It seemed small in his bulky hands. "If Striker is gone, my family will suffer."

"Ah, clever man." Troy observed with distaste. "In that case, we shall have to overcome you."

Ike's expression grew uncertain as the men approached him.

"We do not have much time. Stand here, yes, just so, and I will push against you."

Ike stepped back to keep his balance.

"Good!" Troy backed up and Ike stumbled forward a step. "The tracks look very nice now. It was a good scuffle." Reaching for the sword, Troy grabbed it at the hilt below the blade and above Ike's big hand. "There, now see how I twist it? I am wrenching the weapon from your hand. There is no way you can resist my strength."

Confused, Ike let Troy take the sword and toss it aside. Striker's hand dropped to his side. Startled, he looked up to see Clance working the lock of the second cuff with a tiny metal bar. He had been so caught up in the drama Troy was putting on, that he had not felt Clance at work on his numb hands.

Opening and shutting his free hand, Striker worked the blood back into his fingertips. His left hand fell free, and Striker stifled a cry of pain. Cradling it, he massaged it very gently with his right hand. Clance moved to the lock on the cage. Past him, Ike and Troy were rolling in the dirt in a slow motion wrestling match.

"There now, I've overpowered you," Troy declared, offering his hand to Ike who accepted the help as he got to his feet once more.

"Now what?" the big man boomed in an attempted whisper.

"Now we put you in the cage."

Ike looked doubtfully at the opening Striker was being helped through. "That won't be natural. How could you restrain me in the cage before getting Striker out?" He beamed triumphantly at his wise escape.

"He has a point," Clance agreed, gently rubbing Striker's throbbing hand.

"Tie him up then. We must get the boy away from here at once. His life is in danger. It may be that the uncle has realized that if he kills the king and his son, he would be the next logical ruler even without the boy."

"You must leave me here and warn them at the castle," Striker instructed, flexing his fingers. The painful tingling sensation was fading.

Troy, who had been securing Ike with the old rope he had found, looked up. "Are you crazy? After I battled with all my strength for my freedom?"

"Be serious, Troy. The boy is right. We must warn them before it is too late. But you are also right." Clance put up a hand to stop Troy's objection. "You are also right, we cannot leave the boy to be recaptured."

"The Forbidden Forest. It is not far from here." Troy finished with the rope. "How does that feel?" He asked Ike close to the big man's ear.

"So tight I cannot get out on my own." Ike agreed. "May the Almighty go with you." Seeing Troy's questioning frown, Ike added, "I see His light in you. Why else would I let a skinny runt overpower me?" Ike's grin was contagious. "Now get out of here while you have the chance."

"Thank you, and no matter what he says to you, do not drink the tea!" Troy gave him a pat on the shoulder and hurried to join Clance who pointed Striker towards the Forbidden Forest. They had a good amount of ground to cover and would have to hurry if they wanted to reach the trees before Uncle Harron's men caught up with them.

"But the legends," Striker protested wearily as they picked up the pace.

"The legends are better than the uncle," Troy observed gently. "Erastus will meet you if you stay on the trail. There is no one who knows the forest better than he."

"There is a trail?" Striker wished he had been braver in his threats to enter the forest before.

"You must listen carefully."

A shout from the direction of the cage interrupted Troy's instructions and propelled them into a light jog.

"It is a trail of ferns."

"The forest floor is covered with ferns," Striker informed him. "I have been at the edge of the forest many times."

"Listen, the time is short. We can discuss foliage later if we get through this," Clance put in.

More shouts were heard as others joined in the pursuit behind them. "The ferns are of a type that does not spread on its own. You will know them because their leaves all turn down into a curl. The native ferns arch, but these curl." Troy tried to read the purple side of the young prince's face as they ran. "Do you understand? You have to keep the curled ferns in your path if you want to make it to Emmery's."

"Emmery?" Striker stopped stunned.

Clance put a hand on Striker's upper arm to move him forward but Striker instinctively shook himself free.

"I will not tell you another word about the trail until you start moving. Are you trying to get us all killed?" Troy demanded.

"Be patient with him, Troy," Clance warned. "He is right, Sire, you must keep moving. If they catch you now, I fear for your life."

Stunned by the news and the honored title Clance had used, Striker blinked at them dumbly.

"Forgive me," Clance grasped Striker by the wrist, and the young man fell in step like a well-trained dog.

They were nearing the forest, when Striker tugged his wrist free. He was keeping up now and there was no reason for Clance to hold onto him.

"I thought Emmery was dead," Striker observed.

"She was in grave danger, Sire. As a witness to your birth she had to be protected."

"And I?"

"You will understand it better when there is time to explain," Troy promised, leading the way with confidence into the Forbidden Forest. They walked for several minutes in silence before Troy stepped aside.

"There you are. That is the fern you must follow. If you lose sight of it or stray from it you place yourself in grave danger, for the forest is full of hidden dangers."

Clance bowed respectfully. "May the Almighty go with you."

Troy's bow was slight, as if to an equal.

"Follow the ferns. We must go and warn the king."

Dashing off to the right in the direction of the castle, they ran hard through the uncurled ferns and brush with surprising agility.

———————

"Harron, your plan is falling apart. I told you a year ago it was time to make your move." Laden stood with his arms crossed, blocking the closed door of Uncle Harron's cottage.

"I hope you will not forget your place so easily when you are promoted." Uncle Harron's eyes were narrow and threatening.

"Uncle Harron then, does it really matter now?" Laden spat angrily. "You will be nothing if this plan falls through. Except, perhaps, dead for treason."

Unmoved by his outburst, Uncle Harron continued gathering his things and placing them into the open leather bag on the table. These were the items he would need when he went to see the king. The poison tea was folded into a paper sleeve and tucked securely among the other items. That was to be his last resort if the King and Prince could not be brought to see reason.

"All will come out as it should, Laden," Uncle Harron reassured with a chilling calm. "You will see that I was right in my timing. The boy's disappearance is only temporary. He will be brought to the castle by those Oreathians, and I will be there to meet them." Looking around the room as if for the last time, Uncle Harron nodded. Yes, all was as it should be.

CHAPTER 13

Striker had no idea how long he had been running. His head ached and his mouth was dry, but he did not dare to leave the fern path he followed. The ground beneath his feet was solid and though he had to pause for breath, there were no obstacles to be avoided.

After a few more minutes, Striker slowed to a walk, the ferns dragging at his ankles as if trying to hold him back from something ahead.

Where was this Erastus, his so called guardian who rarely appeared when needed? If that was who the name belonged to. Striker sank into thought. Troy had called him Sire. They believed he was the prince of Choi. What a jump to go from the curse of the land to the ruler of it. What did he mean when he said Striker would understand everything once it was explained? Would one little explanation make up for seventeen years of suffering? Striker did not see how it could. Even for a good cause, why could they not have taken him when they took Emmery to safety? Why leave him to be reviled and hated by those he was later to rule?

Without warning, the ground gave way and Striker cried out as he fell. A strong hand grasped Striker's arm, stopping him mid air. Looking down, Striker saw his feet hung over a dark abyss below.

"Give me your other hand."

Striker knew the deep voice at once. Above him was the

man from the field, the one who had given him hope in the form of a tiny wooden hawk. Moving carefully, Striker raised his other hand above his head and once more felt the strong grip of the stranger. The man grunted with the effort as he dragged Striker back up onto solid ground.

"You left the path." It was not an accusation, only an explanation to clear the confused look Striker wore.

Looking around, Striker found he was right. While his mind was lost in thought, his feet had wandered from the trail of ferns.

"Thank you." Striker peered back down the deep hole. "That was close."

Though the man smiled, his eyes held a warning.

"I suppose you are Erastus." Rubbing his wrist cuffs, Striker moved back to where the curled ferns grew.

"That is correct. Do you mind if I travel with you?" the stranger asked without following.

"You are always asking if I mind things." Striker boldly met Erastus' gaze. "What if I minded being left to grow up in Choi?"

Erastus nodded slowly. "It was a hard thing to bear."

"That is obvious enough."

"We should keep moving."

"Where are we going?"

"You trusted Troy and Clance but do not trust me," Erastus observed quietly.

"Why should I? They got me out as soon as they could. You could have gotten me out but did not." Striker stood his ground.

"In the woods you would have learned to survive," Erastus paused and added, "If you survived. Your mother was almost killed before we could find her."

"But you let her die," Striker observed coolly.

A sad look passed over Erastus' face and he did not

respond. Striker was sorry he had said it. All the man had ever done was help him. Why was it so hard to trust him?

"You were the one who saved her," Striker said after a long silence.

"I tried to save her." Erastus looked away, trying to master the emotions that accompanied the memory.

"Will you tell me about it?" Striker asked, moving forward on the path once more.

With a nod, Erastus fell in step with Striker. "You have a right to know. After she ran away, we never stopped searching for Elise. For eight and a half months we combed the forest, lowering men into every pit, searching through every clump of brush, fighting though tangles of thorns."

"Why were you looking so hard? Did Prince Deetry send you?" Striker asked. He noticed the trees were becoming much larger than the ones he had passed before. Their branches closed in above them to shut out the sunlight.

"No, Deetry's scouts did not look long. The prince's father called off the search after only a week. Princess Elise is the daughter of our king. We came to find her because the love of her father still held onto hope."

Nodding thoughtfully, Striker waited for him to go on.

"She was dying when I found her. She recognized me, I saw it in her eyes, but she was too weak to speak. I knew at once, by the look in her eyes, that there was nothing that could be done to save her. Even as she lingered near death, the time came for you to be born."

Striker knew the town's version of the story, but hearing it from Erastus it all made sense.

"I am a soldier, and my medical knowledge is limited. She was so weak, I knew that I had to get her to help. Emmery knew of our searches. Her house was nearby and she often entered the fringes of the forest to gather healing herbs. I carried Princess Elise." Erastus' eyes grew sad with the memory and his voice softened until Striker could barely make out his words. "She was so light. So frail. Deep inside, I knew that the princess I had sworn to protect was nearly gone."

―――――――――

"Will your father send men to help us take the throne for Oreathia?" Clance asked softly.

Troy glanced at his companion and sighed. They were making their way towards the great river that separated the little town of Choi from the palace. Some time ago, to avoid the sentries along the way, they had left the road to travel along the animal trails that curved through the dense woods towards the river.

"What does that mean, Troy?" Clance paused but hurried to catch up when Troy did not slow. "We are on our own then?"

"You knew it when we set out, Clance," Troy finally answered solemnly. "The gravity of our mission is sinking in now that the boy is freed and the rush of adventure has worn away." Troy hoped the young prince would stick with Erastus and follow the plan. They needed him to prove Harron was a threat to the king.

"I did not come for the adventure." Clance pointed out, breaking into Troy's thoughts.

This time, Troy's glance was accompanied by a grin. "You are a faithful friend, Clance."

Clance did not respond. A call from the guard had drawn his attention.

Uncle Harron had passed on the road not long before. He was saluted by the guards and would gain access to the king long before they had reached the castle. Troy's head rose and he squared his shoulders against the heavy weight of the kingdom that rested on him. Not his own kingdom.

Oreathia was to be wisely ruled by his older brother, the first son of his father. No, it was the kingdom of Choi that hung on the brink of destruction. If a man like Harron weaseled his way into power, Choi would quickly fall under his selfish leadership.

The king of Oreathia could not send an army to force King Deetrin to accept his grandson's right to the throne of Choi. That would be a sure call for war. King Deetrin was a shrewd king and had many allies that would come quickly to his aid. No, if it was to be done, the choice to accept the prince they knew as Striker must be left to King Deetrin and the boy's father, Prince Deetry.

———————

They had walked in silence for some time when Striker asked, "You said my mother was already gone when you were carrying her. How did she get to the cottage if she was already gone?"

"She was not dead yet, but so weak that there was barely a hint of the princess I knew. The moment I found her, I knew that she would not survive the trip back to her own land. As I said before, her only chance and your only hope of survival, was for me to get her into the hands of an experienced midwife or doctor. I carried your mother to the edge of the wood where there were people who could help her. There was much unrest between your kingdom and mine because of the forbidden marriage. To be seen carrying the dying princess, even in the plain uniform of my country, would have been very dangerous."

"But you said she was already dying," Striker observed. The curled ferns wove in and out in a maddeningly indirect path. The movement deeper into the forest was considerably slower than if one could have walked in a straight line towards its heart.

"Yes, but you were not," Erastus pointed out. "To bring her as the princess, would endanger you as the future king of Choi and the submissive realms beyond. The old king had only to kill you, a helpless infant, and his kingdom would be freed from its truce by marriage with my country. To reveal your true identity would have put you in the gravest danger. The king would have stopped at nothing to have you killed. Even the dangers of the forest would not keep him from pursuing you. And, if the only son of my King's beloved princess was killed, war between the lands would be inevitable." Erastus glanced at Striker now and then to see if he was following the reasoning. Because Erastus was walking on Striker's left, he could not see the fading purple dye. Erastus had accompanied Princess Elise to the Choian palace and had occasion to see Prince Deetry many times during their courtship. The boy's serious face was so like Prince Deetry's. Even his expressions plainly revealed his royal blood. Erastus wondered that no one had seen it before.

"But you could have hidden me here."

"Yes, but the trails were not marked then," Erastus answered. He slowed and scanned the underbrush. "There, to the left. The path turns sharply here. See the curled ferns? This turn is not well marked in order to protect Emmery should someone discover the secret of the trail." Erastus walked on boldly, and Striker fell in step beside him once more. "As I was saying, if you lived here you would grow up a wild man, with no knowledge of how to interact with people, or how a kingdom was run. You would have hated and feared your people instead of knowing them and their needs as you do now. That is, of course, if you had survived the forest. On the other hand, to hide you under their noses and to pretend you were a curse, allowed you to live and grow."

"So you are working with Uncle Harron?" Striker knew

the answer he desperately wanted to hear.

"No. It was Harron's own greed that got in the way." Erastus saw Striker's shoulders sink with relief. "Harron used the legend of the curse for his own purposes. He started inflicting curses on people to strengthen his position as the caretaker of the curse. Harron, emboldened by his taste of power, threatened that he would tell the king if Emmery did not follow his plan. He became dangerous. That is why Emmery was taken to safety."

Striker stopped walking "And me? If you knew he was dangerous, why did you leave me?"

"Once you were out of his power, he would have gone straight to the king. There would be a reward for your death. He would have gained less from your death than he would have from your life, but still he would not come away empty handed." Erastus walked on, and Striker moved to his position beside him once more. They took yet another hairpin turn in the path. Striker could see the next path just beyond. However, having fallen into the pit, he was much more careful to follow the trail.

They walked in silence for a minute or two. It was Erastus who spoke first. "There are many things in life that we do, thinking them to be the wisest option at the time. Later, when we have more understanding, we wish for the chance to go back and change them. We did what we thought was best for you without truly knowing how much you suffered," Erastus confessed softly. "You bore the suffering well and instead of embracing bitterness, you became a man I would be honored to serve under."

"But what of my mother?" Striker asked, uncomfortable with where the conversation was going. There was no way to go back and change his past, and he did not want to think about what could have been when it could not ever be now. "You said that you carried her through the forest, and then what?"

"I brought her as near as I dared to the cottage closest to the forest's edge. With a well-placed stone, I roused the house. Standing your mother upright, I let her stumble from the woods into their arms." He looked sad again. "Oh how I wished I had found your mother in time to bring her home to Oreathia. You would have been born there in safety and raised with care." He stopped and met Striker's eyes. "You cannot know how that thought has plagued me over the years. All of your suffering was truly because of my failure."

"But I owe my life to you, Erastus." Striker put out his purple right hand and shook Erastus' hand firmly. "I understand now why it had to be this way. I am grateful for the little comforts you left along the way and for the many times you saved my life."

Erastus' drew Striker into a strong hug. It was a foreign feeling to be restrained by love, even for just a few seconds. Striker forced himself to stand and bear it.

When he stepped back, Striker saw that the eyes of the mighty warrior were moist. "Thank you, Sire. For you to say so is a huge weight lifted." Erastus looked down quickly. "Forgive my boldness, Sire."

"Oh." Striker cleared his throat. He tried to remember if anyone had ever apologized to him before. "Of course you are forgiven." Uncomfortable with the emotional situation, Striker looked around. "I have only one more question. Where are we going? It will take a week of Sundays to get back to the castle."

Erastus' laugh boomed across the stillness of the wood. "We are going to see Emmery and to take her back to the palace to prove to your father that you are indeed his son, and his heir by rights of relation."

CHAPTER 14

"Pa, what are you doing?" Hans stood in the doorway surveying his father's blacksmith shop.

"I have an errand at the castle," Ike boomed in response, adding a hammer to his large leather shoulder bag. Ike looked his son over and nodded. "You may come if you are quiet and stay out of trouble."

"But what errand do you have?" Hans demanded. "Are you truly going to the castle?"

"My son," Ike moved some straw from the top of an old chest. He paused, crouching there in the dirt, and looked up at his oldest son. "If you are quiet," the big man's look was meaningful, "and stay out of trouble, you may come. I could use your help with the tools."

"But, Pa."

Seeing the look on his father's weathered face, Hans shut his mouth and said no more. His eyes grew wide as Ike opened the trunk revealing several gleaming swords. He chose four of them. Each blade was quickly inspected before it was carefully wrapped in a piece of thick cloth. When he was satisfied, the blacksmith slid the swords into his bag.

"Pa," Hans breathed in alarm.

"If you spent less time playing with the other boys and more time learning your trade, you would know a blacksmith does more than pound out shoes for horses and sharpen plows."

"But swords are expressly forbidden," Hans hissed moving closer to his father. The years of pounding steel had made a private conversation with his father impossible. There was no telling who would be passing outside the blacksmith shop. Forbidden swords were hardly something to be shouted about in the middle of the town.

"What?" Ike's eyes betrayed the fact that he had heard his son's words. "I sharpen things for farmers and workers. I accept tools of all trades." He met Hans' eyes for an instant. Gesturing to the bag he held, he asked, "Are these not tools of a trade?"

Hans' frown remained but he nodded in agreement. "They are."

"Good, it is time we started. We must reach the castle soon if we are to be of any help to the king."

————————

"Uncle Harron, to what do we owe this honor?" King Deetrin beckoned to a servant who brought a cushioned chair for their guest and placed it at the table near the king.

Uncle Harron took his seat and looked down the table at Prince Deetry, who smiled politely to conceal his distaste for their unexpected guest.

"Bring our guest a plate. He will join us for dinner," the king instructed. "Unless of course your news is too urgent to allow it." He was very aware of how much his advisor enjoyed the finer things of life at the palace.

Uncle Harron's head dipped down briefly in thanks. "I would be honored to join your majesties."

"Is all well in the village of Choi?" Prince Deetry asked. Despite the years that had passed, he could not give up the hope that somehow news would come of his bride. He was a well-treated prisoner inside his father's castle, and often wondered if the king feared the reappearance of Elise as much as his son desired it.

Giving the prince an oily smile, Uncle Harron once again marveled at the similarity between Striker and the prince before him. "Yes, Sire, all is well." In the last year, the boy had changed so much that there were times Uncle Harron feared someone would discover his identity. Even Laden was chaffing at the possibility of losing everything to one gossip with a loose tongue. There was no doubt that Prince Deetry and Striker were related.

Uncle Harron moved slightly to allow the plate to be set before him. He waved the servant away, privately considering his options. He could kill both the prince and the king, leaving Striker to rule under his command. This would be tricky, now that the boy knew of his heritage. There was the option of killing the old king and blackmailing Deetry to give up the throne in order to save his son's life. However, if the prince gained power and returned, Harron would find himself in a delicate position. No, the best option would be to remove Prince Deetry. The old king would happily pass his kingdom on to Harron if the only other option would be to give it to the grandchild he hated so fiercely. If he did not, Harron would forgive him over a cup of strong tea.

Harron smiled as the servants brought platters of food into the hall. There was no rush. He would enjoy one last meal at the king's expense. In good time, the boy would be brought to the palace by loyal subjects who thought to aid him in becoming the next king. They would think themselves clever, only to find Uncle Harron has already laid a trap for them. The battle that would follow their arrival would lead to the untimely death of Prince Deetry. The captain of the guard would see to it personally. It happened that the captain was also a man of high taste who desired a title and lands beyond his current position. Until Striker appeared,

Uncle Harron would enjoy the rich foods that would soon be his usual fare.

———————

Troy strode up to the palace gate. "I am Troy, second son of his majesty, the King of Oreathia. I request an audience with the king. His life is in danger."

"In danger from whom, you?" the guard asked without bothering to stand at attention in the presence of the allied prince. "You will not get past this gate. Uncle Harron has already warned us about your plot to pose as the prince of Oreathia and assassinate the king."

Troy frowned. "My good man, see here the royal sealing ring on my finger. And here is an official letter from my father the king requesting I am given audience."

"Still sore about the runaway princess all these years later, are we?" The guard signaled to three other guards and they moved to join him. "We have a reception planned for you, your highness. Uncle Harron arranged it all in the highest of styles." The speaker gave a nod, and the other guards fanned out. One grabbed Troy by the arm. In the same instant, his breath caught and he crumpled to the ground.

"Stay back, all of you," Troy warned, snatching up the unconscious man's sword. "For the good of your country stay back."

Another guard rushed him, and he too fell suddenly with no apparent wound.

"It is black magic," the remaining guard murmured, backing away from Troy.

"It is Harron who is even now seeking the death of your king. Send a messenger if you do not believe me," Troy pleaded urgently. "What harm could it do? Harron has created a poisonous tea. He wishes to remove the royal family from the throne. If you do not listen and they are killed, their blood will be on your head."

"Go and see that the king is in good health," the guard ordered a fresh-faced page lingering inside the gate. The boy, convinced that the stranger spoke the truth, ran to carry out his orders.

"Are you happy now?" the guard asked with a jeer. "Now go home before we arrest you." They had already tried, but he did not mention that fact.

"I will see your king." Troy lunged with his sword, crossing blades with the guard. "His life is in grave danger. If you will not fight for him, I will, for our kingdoms are allied by marriage."

The remaining guard rushed forward once more.

Out of sight, Clance drew back the stone in his crossbow and aimed it once more.

"But why take me so deep into the forest, Erastus?" Striker asked impatiently. "Would it not be easier to bring Emmery to the castle?"

Erastus smiled. "Surely, you are not tiring, Sire."

Striker looked hard at the ground.

When he did not answer, Erastus glanced back. Even under the uneven mop of hair Striker tried to hide behind, Erastus could see the young man's mouth was screwed up to keep back his emotions.

"What is it, Sire?" Erastus, who had been walking ahead for a time, went back to walk beside Striker. "Are you well?"

"What if…," a half-choked sob escaped him and he turned away so Erastus would not see his tears. A few moments passed in silence. After a shaky breath, Striker wiped his eyes with the back of his hand and tried again, "What if Uncle

Harron kills my father before I can meet him?" Again he turned from Erastus as his emotions swelled.

Erastus's eyes were moist as he once more pulled Striker into a hug. This time, the young man leaned into it. His body trembled as he took a long breath.

After a few moments, Erastus held Striker at arm's length and looked him in the eye. "I cannot promise you that your father will be safe. But I know that Prince Troy and Clance will do everything in their power to protect him."

Striker nodded without speaking.

"We must go on. It is not much farther now. Can you manage?"

"Yes." Striker started off, following the ferns with a new determination. Already he was shedding the slinking, haunted behavior of one who has been treated badly. He walked erect, confident, as Erastus had often seen Striker walk when he was alone. By the grace of the Almighty, the life of pain had not squelched the greatness in him. He had responded to it all without bitterness, and Erastus knew this young man would be the best king Choi had ever had. He had only to get the young prince safely to his place on the throne before it was too late.

CHAPTER 15

"I would not fret about the man at the gate, Your Highnesses. There have often been travelers who wish to gain an audience by lies." Uncle Harron's voice was soothing. "Your guards are well trained and will take care of them quickly."

Across the table, Prince Deetry eyed Harron with distrust.

"Deetry, go and see what it is about," the King ordered. "I must retire and rest. That page, bursting in with news of my life being in danger, gave my poor old heart a jolt. To think, they accused you, Harron, my trusted adviser." The king laughed weakly.

Harron shook his head. "I would rather die myself than see any harm come to you, Your Highness," Harron lied with a slight bow of his head. He carried with him the ingredients to kill the old king under the guise of a harmless cup of tea.

"Good to hear." The king was helped to his feet by his aid. "Any man who dared to consider my demise or to voice a claim to my throne would be killed immediately."

"As they should be." Harron's agreement was tainted with the realization that the King would never give his kingdom to Harron if he were threatened. Prince Deetry would soon be battling for his life with the captain. Harron would have to get rid of the old king now or he could lose everything. For an instant, he wondered if Laden had been right when he accused Harron of holding his cards too long.

"Harron, are you feeling well?" The knowing look in the

king's eyes reminded Harron of when the king was a younger, more worthy opponent.

"Yes, Sire. I cannot help to be saddened by the accusation that I would bring any harm to your highness." Harron took a deep breath, pretending to put the thought out of his mind. "You are tired, Sire, perhaps some warm refreshment would help to calm your nerves?"

"Yes, Harron, bring me some tea. You can prepare it in my chamber while I am settled into bed. Your herbs are very soothing."

After a deeper bow to the king, Harron ordered a servant to fetch a kettle of hot water for the king's tea. As the man hurried to obey, Harron calmly followed the king to his chambers.

Movement on the parapet above caught Troy's eye, and he sprinted in close to the wall where the archer would have to reveal himself in order to aim a shot at him below. An arrow glanced off the stones an arm's length to his right. The archer was not aiming. He had seen the fate of his comrades below, and yet he had allowed Troy to approach to the wall.

Troy looked towards where he knew Clance was hiding and cocked his head towards the wall. A moment later the archer's bow, and the arrow that was on his string, clattered to the stone pavement beside Troy.

Touching his fingertips briefly to his forehead in salute, Troy picked up the bow and arrow. He had no other option than to carry them in his left hand. The sword would serve him better in close quarters.

Three stones flew through the air in quick succession. Two of them cracked against the parapet and rained down on Troy.

Clance sprinted across the open courtyard to where Troy stood against the wall. "Apologies, Troy, I did not aim them well in my haste."

"You have not hit me yet." Troy observed with a grin. "I'll give you another chance at it inside."

Clance's eyes were running over the strong gate. It was no doubt barred from inside. They had very little chance of getting in, and the guards he had knocked down would rouse soon. "What now?"

Uncertain, Troy put out his hand to try the handle of the door beside the gate. They looked at each other in astonishment as it opened beneath his hand.

"The king is in good health. He…" The page saw them too late and was not strong enough to hold the door against them.

Pushing their way in, Clance grabbed the fleeing boy by the arm. "Where is the king?"

"I cannot tell you." His boyish eyes were full of fear. "Please do not hurt me."

"What is your name?"

"My name is Jake. Please do not kill me." The boy trembled in Clance's strong grasp.

Turning his attention from the strangely empty castle grounds, Clance looked into the boy's terrified eyes. "Jake, I will not hurt you if you will take me to King Deetrin."

The page stood taller and met Clance's gaze like a man. "I cannot betray my king even for my life."

Troy gestured, and Clance moved along the inside of the wall toward his companion. His grip on the page remained firm. "I hope the king realizes what a fine, young man he has in his service," Clance observed seriously. "You are not betraying your king, Jake. You are saving his life. Even you must see that Harron is a threat."

"Uncle Harron has never hurt the king before and has been

alone with him many times." Jake lifted his chin stubbornly.

An arrow narrowly missed Troy, and the three of them scrambled for cover. Newly unloaded barrels still sitting beside the empty supply wagon offered the protection they needed. The heavy footfalls of Choian soldiers echoed in the courtyard as the Oreathians ducked out of sight.

Jake, pulled down beside Troy, heard him mutter. "I was a fool."

"What have you done?" Jake asked tentatively.

"I am the prince of Oreathia. I could have come with an escort, boldly come to have an audience with the king. Then I would have been admitted at once. I was too afraid I would endanger the Striker. This foolishness is of my own doing. I only pray it does not cost the king his life."

"But with an escort you would have never made it into the town of Choi." Clance pointed out, trying to gauge the number of soldiers who were assembling across the stone court. "Lesser Choi is a well-guarded secret. What use would it have been to be welcomed into the castle before the Striker was rescued?"

They ducked as another arrow embedded itself in one of the barrels. A dark sticky liquid began to seep from the barrel where the arrow had pierced it. Troy silently wondered if the molasses oozing from the split wood was a symbol of how the battle would end. He took a breath to steady himself. Meeting Clance's gaze, he knew his companion shared his thoughts. They could not afford to be beaten in their minds before the battle had begun. "With the help of the Almighty we must save the king," Troy told Clance and Jake seriously. "If we fail, and Harron takes the throne, Oreathia and Choi will surely go to war. Many will be killed in a battle we could have prevented."

Clance nodded once, his resolve firm once more. Jake squirmed uncomfortably in the stranger's grasp.

"Strangers, and enemies of our king, by order of His Majesty, Deetrian, king of Choi, I command you to throw out your weapons and surrender," the commander bellowed across the empty courtyard.

"We are here not to harm your king but to warn him that his life is in danger," Troy boldly shouted back.

An arrow struck the metal band of the barrel Troy hid behind. Glancing off, it fell to the pavement with a clatter. Silence followed.

"They are not trying to kill us, Troy. They are holding us here, keeping us under cover with their arrows. Could they know that the Striker will be brought to the palace?"

Troy's mouth was a hard line. Clance only had a few arrows left. If the soldiers stood with Harron, there would be very little they could do to protect the young prince from ten well-trained soldiers.

"For the Almighty and Oreathia," Clance hissed to Troy. Before Troy could protest, Clance loaded an arrow in his crossbow and sent it expertly across the courtyard. It glanced off the guard's shield at an angle and harmlessly struck another man nearby as it fell to the ground. The shot had the desired effect. As the castle guard dove for cover, Clance sprinted across the open space and leapt over the low wall of the stable yard. The page, anticipating the Oreathian's move, clambered over the wall right behind him.

Clance looked into the wide, scared eyes of the page beside him, "If you love your country, Jake, you must help us warn the king. His life is in grave danger."

CHAPTER 16

"Emmery, I brought the prince," Erastus called.

Striker looked around but saw no one. There was not even a house in sight. There were only trees and ferns just like he had seen for what seemed like hours.

Erastus scanned the area for any sign of danger. "Emmery, we must hurry."

A clump of ferns with a peculiar red leaved plant growing among them caught Striker's eyes. As he watched, it seemed as if that clump rose out of the ground.

"Erastus, look," Striker pointed to the ferns that were quickly rising higher.

Erastus smiled. "I see."

The ferns rose until they were perpendicular to the ground. Beneath them, a plump, wrinkled woman appeared. Striker stared in amazement. The ferns were planted in a trap door the old lady had opened from below.

"Hello." She stopped and looked at Erastus then back at Striker. "I know who you are, but I do not know your name."

"Striker." Even as he said it, Striker felt ashamed. Emmery was the one who had christened him. But he was not the only one who had suffered. Here was a skilled woman who was forced to live like an animal underground because he had been born. Uncle Harron was right. So many people had been made to suffer because Striker had not died along with his mother in the woods 17 years ago.

Emmery must have read his thoughts in his face. She pushed the fern door aside where it rested softly against a nearby tree. Climbing the steep, wooden steps, she emerged and knelt before him.

"You are not a burden Striker. You do not bring pain."

He bit his lip but said nothing.

"The Almighty sent you to save Choi. Harron means to bring this town and all the countries under King Deetrin's rule under his own power. You are the rightful heir, and you were saved for a purpose. You must never let anyone tell you otherwise."

He nodded, but she could see he did not believe her. "I'm not a warrior, Emmery. I would be useless in a battle and I fear I am already too late to help them." Putting out his hand, he helped the old midwife to her feet. "Would it not be better for us all if I went into hiding as you did?"

Emmery stood but did not release his hand.

He looked at her, his eyes puzzled.

"You are the rightful heir, Prince Deetrith," she repeated. "Is not trying to save your father and failing, better than not trying at all?"

Striker nodded slowly. The name she had called him had awakened something inside of him that he did not understand. "Yes," he said thoughtfully. His voice grew firm as he spoke. "I will go with you, and Erastus, but on one condition."

Emmery and Erastus glanced at one another. "And what is your condition?"

"You must never call me by that name again." Striker's chin rose and he stood before them with confidence. For a moment, he looked exactly like his father, Prince Deetry.

"But it is the name of royalty, Sire." Emmery pointed out "The name passed on from king to king in Choi. Your name is Deetrith, son of Prince Deetry and rightful heir to the throne of Choi."

"That may be the tradition, but I am not a full Choian, am I? I will not be called Deet anything. It is a poor name and much overused." Striker ducked his head and quickly added "No disrespect to the king, or m…my father, of course."

"What are we to call you, Sire?" Erastus asked, seeing Emmery was at a loss for words.

"Javen. I was called this before by someone who looked past the curse and saw me. I wish to keep that name."

"Come then, Prince Javen, we do not have much time." Emmery gathered her skirts and descended the stairs into the dim, gaping hole in the ground. "I heard the alarm and the first sounds of battle through the tunnel."

"The tunnel?" Striker asked, looking at Erastus for explanation.

"Yes, there is a tunnel. That is why we came here. It is sheltered and will take us back much faster than we came. Quickly, there is no time to talk. I will explain as we go."

Striker followed her hesitantly and heard Erastus coming behind him.

"I am sorry you have no experience with a sword, Prince Javen," Erastus said from above. "That would have come in handy right about now."

"No use crying over what you do not have," Emmery pointed out. "And you, Prince Javen, stop thinking of yourself as Striker. You may not want to bear the royal name but you are still the rightful heir of Choi."

"I thought Choi was just a town." Javen looked around the cozy, little room they had entered. It reminded him strongly of the widow Zina's home. He shook his head to clear it, refusing to relive the memory of her death.

"Oh, no, Choi is a country. This town is called Choi, or Lesser Choi, because it is technically a part of the capital city." Bustling about, Emmery brought two small cloth bundles from an herb-cluttered, wooden counter. Above the slab of wood, bunches of dried spices hung from pegs in the wall.

"I have lived there all my life and never heard of another Choi," Javen pointed out. He looked up as Erastus pulled the trap door closed above them. For the first time, he noticed there was a soft green light coming from several places further into the room.

"You did not hear of it because Uncle Harron forbids the mention of Greater Choi in your presence. He said it would bring a curse on the capital city." Erastus paused on the bottom step of the ladder and frowned thoughtfully. "Or was it the royal family?" He gave a little shrug, dismissing the thought, and went on. "The point is, Uncle Harron would do anything to keep you from knowing of your father before his time came to step into power and claim the throne."

"We must start for the castle. This is yours." Emmery handed Javen one of the bundles and the other to Erastus. "You will eat much better once you are with your father, Prince Javen, but this will hold you over until then." She crossed the crowded room once more to retrieve a third bundle.

The smell of the food inside the cloth made Javen's stomach growl.

Glancing reproachfully at Erastus, Emmery asked, "He did not feed you?"

"We were fleeing for our lives, Emmery," Erastus responded, unlatching a door in the wall to their right. "We did not have time to find food."

"I didn't say anything to you, Erastus," Emmery answered with twinkling eyes. "Prince Javen, Choi is a large city on the other side of the castle. Emmery was deftly choosing helpful herbs to bring along. "Much of the produce of Lesser Choi goes to the markets in the big city. The river serves as a barrier between Choi and Lesser Choi where you grew up."

"I did not know there was a river." Javen was painfully aware of his ignorance of the outside world. "I was never allowed to go in the direction of the palace."

Emmery went on with her explanation with no mention of whether or not the prince should have known about the river before now. "The river that runs beneath the castle bridge is strong and dangerous. Years ago, farmers from Lesser Choi were looked down on by those who lived in the city of Choi. Over time, this, along with Uncle Harron's threats, caused the farmers to stop going into Choi altogether. Now, people do not cross from town to city. Only on the yearly celebration do the people from Choi cross the great bridge. Though passage to the castle gate is permitted if requested, rarely are people permitted to go inside."

Erastus continued the narrative. "The unguarded way between the town and the city is the road out of your Choi which you were forbidden to travel." Taking a sheathed sword and belt from the top of Emmery's cupboard, he deftly strapped it around his waist. "Harron scared the townspeople of Choi well enough with his stories about the curse that Laden was the only farmer who ever traveled to the greater side of Choi. The other farmers sent their goods with him."

As they talked, Emmery had packed the herbs and medical supplies into a homemade bag which hung at her side. Looking one last time around the room, she declared, "We are ready."

CHAPTER 17

"I am here to check the shoes of the king's army horses," Ike bellowed up at the sentry.

"Do you have a royal summons?" the gatekeeper asked, wishing he was inside with all the action.

"No, if I had one it would be at home." Even after years of living in Choi, Ike's thick accent remained. "My task is very important. Choi rumbles with rumors about the Oreathian king. I came as quickly as I could. In my haste I did not bring a summons."

The king's man retreated out of sight.

"Do you have a summons?" Hans asked close to his father's ear.

"If I did, it would be at home," Ike repeated, his eyes laughing, "Because it is not with me."

"Boy, what is in that bag you have?"

Hans did not hesitate, "Tools of a trade, Sir."

"Hammers and things, I suppose." The gatekeeper pressed with little interest.

"Those are the tools of my father's trade." Hans responded honestly.

"This is not a good time, tradesmen. Come back tomorrow."

"Tomorrow would be too late," Ike boomed. "I can hear the noise of battle inside the courtyard and can tell by your attention that it is a close match. If the king's horses are poorly shod, it could cost him the victory should he need to go and face the army of Oreathia. Is it not true that the Choian army has left the castle unguarded to face an enemy to the west?"

The sentry looked at the pair standing at the gate below him as if seeing them for the first time. "You know a lot about the affairs of the kingdom for a country blacksmith."

"I love my king." Ike said by way of explanation.

Hans shifted the strap of the bag on his shoulder.

"The bag is heavy for the boy. If the king's safety and urgent summons mean nothing to you, we will return to Choi. The lives of peasants change very little with the conquering of a new king."

"I have seen you here before," The guard confessed. He had no desire to argue with a peasant when there were intruders battling the guard inside the courtyard. It was true that the army had departed, and believable that the king would have summoned the blacksmith to see to the horses left behind. Torn, he hesitated a moment more before shouting down for the gate to be opened. "See that you go straight to the stable. And stay out of the main courtyard," the guard ordered.

Ike bowed slightly in submission and thanks. Hans noticed his father had not actually agreed to the gatekeeper's terms.

"Hold your fire." A tall, dark haired young man strode from one of the open doors.

He was recognized at once, and the captain shouted the order to his men.

The handful of guards assembled in a respectful line before their prince, while keeping a wary eye on where the intruders were hiding. Beyond the one misfired arrow, the Oreathians had not attacked them, but the Choian guard would be ready if they did.

"Where are the Oreathians who have come to see my

father?" Prince Deetry inquired.

"There, Your Highness, behind those barrels is the one who claims to be a prince. His friend is behind that low wall by the blacksmith station."

Prince Deetry dismissed him with a nod. "Please friends, come out of hiding. Word has reached me that you have come from Oreathia to warn my father and me of an unknown danger. What is it you have come to say?"

Troy stood slowly knowing one arrow could end his life.

From his hiding place, Clance silently loaded an arrow into his crossbow.

"You must not kill the prince!" Jake scrambled to stand in front of Clance's bow.

Clance set the bow aside and grabbed Jake firmly by the shoulders. Pulling the boy down behind the safety of the low wall, he spoke in a quick, low tone. "I would not dare to harm your prince or your king. You must trust me. Oreathia is an ally of Choi and we have come to save your king, not to kill him." Clance glanced past him at Troy who stood exposed before the Choian soldiers, then met Jake's eyes once more. "You must trust me."

Releasing him, Clance once more picked up his bow. Jake moved aside and crouched beside the Oreathian.

With his sword in hand, Troy walked across the open courtyard toward Prince Deetry whose own blade hung in its sheath at his side.

The guards surged forward to defend their prince.

"Let him come," Prince Deetry ordered firmly.

Unsure, they glanced at their captain.

Prince Deetry turned on them, his eyes blazing with anger. "Would you question me? Would you look to the authority of your captain over mine? You are not worthy to stand in my defense if my authority holds so low of a place in your eyes."

They cringed before him. Several dropped to one knee, begging his pardon.

Prince Deetry looked hard at them. "I will let it go this time as an error of judgment in the pressure of the moment. If you ever question my authority again, you will find yourself imprisoned as traitors of the crown."

"Yes, Your Highness." Those who had knelt stood quickly and joined their comrades in a crisp salute to their future king. Not one dared to look away from his calculating gaze.

Turning to Troy, Prince Deetry waited.

"Harron has come to kill your father, and you, Prince Deetry. He has concocted a poisonous tea. You must not let him give that tea to your father. You must go to your father at once, Sire. Do not drink or eat anything Harron offers."

"Uncle Harron is with father now," Prince Deetry's face grew pale as the realization sunk in. He had unknowingly left his father in grave danger. "Captain, bring your men at once!" Prince Deetry spun and ran back towards the door he had emerged from a few minutes before. As the soldiers moved to follow, something flew with a hiss past Troy. In horror they watched as an Oreathian arrow struck the prince, embedding itself deeply in his back. He cried out and fell on the stone steps, only a few feet from the safety of the castle.

"They have murdered the prince!" The captain shouted the alarm. The guards drew their swords and charged.

Jake turned on Clance, his face contorted with rage and pain. "You said…" He stopped. The arrow was still on Clance's bow. He saw the shock in the man's face and knew at once the Oreathian arrow that struck the prince was not shot by an Oreathian but by one of the prince's own guard.

———

Silently Erastus, Emmery, and Javen hurried through the

tunnel towards the castle. The same dim, green light he had seen in Emmery's house gave shape to the walls and floor of the long, straight tunnel. It was wide enough for two people to walk side by side, but they went single file over the hard packed dirt floor. It had been decided that Erastus would go first, in case they were met with any opposition before they reached the castle. Emmery followed behind him leaving Prince Javen in the protected position at the back of their little troop.

The smell of the food Javen carried made him dizzy with hunger. Before, when he was young, he would have eaten it quickly while no one was watching. Over the years he had learned that it was better to have eaten and take the shouting and bitter words that followed than to go hungry in silence. After he had chosen to follow the Almighty, Striker had found that stealing produced a strange disquiet in his heart, as if the Almighty One was not pleased. Widow Zina had said the Almighty would speak to him and if he obeyed he would learn to hear Him better. After that, Javen had chosen to go hungry rather than to steal his food. Now, Emmery and Erastus treated him as royalty. Javen wondered if a good king would steal even a parcel of food from his subjects.

"Can I eat this?" Javen finally asked, after they had walked a ways in silence.

Emmery laughed softly. "He will have to get used to being a prince."

"It will come with practice," Erastus answered softly. He walked ahead with his sword drawn and ready.

Emmery turned back to look at Javen without slowing her pace. He could just make out her face as she passed under a ray of dim, green light. Her smile was kind, and he knew she was not speaking ill of him.

"Of course you may eat it, Your Highness. I made it for you."

"Thank you." He was still having trouble swallowing the new titles being so quickly bestowed on him. Unwrapping their food, they ate the cheese and dried meat in grateful silence as they hurried down the long tunnel. They had just finished when Emmery paused to pick up three wooden canteens from the edge of the tunnel.

"I thought they might be handy right about here." She laughed at their surprised expressions. "I made them myself. The inner coating keeps the water in and also has medicinal purposes. Pull out the cork. You will find it quite refreshing. You can leave the napkins from your meal here. I will pick them up later if we make it out alive."

Erastus's soft laugh echoed down the tunnel. "If we make it out alive, you can leave them here forever, Emmery."

Pushing the cork back into the mouth of his canteen, Javen looked at the backs of his guides. One was tall and muscular, and the other bulky and stooped. "Do you think there is a chance?" His solemn tone silenced the others.

CHAPTER 18

"There, Your Highness, the tea is prepared. You will find this new mixture to be especially soothing." Harron motioned to the attendant who helped the king to sit up, arranging the pillows behind him. Harron himself carried the tray to the king's bedside.

"You have had a terrible start, Your Majesty and you must remember your heart is not as strong as it once was."

"Yes, yes. I can feel it pounding still." The king took the cup and saucer he was handed.

"While it cools, I have a question that I have wanted to ask you for some time."

The king lowered the cup and allowed it to rest on the thick comforter that covered him from the waist down. "What is it, Harron? You seem quite nervous. We have always held open counsel together. Tell me what is bothering you."

"If there was a chance that Elise's child survived…"

The king's face darkened. "There is no chance that there was a child."

"But if there were, Your Highness, would you allow that child, now nearly a man, to rule in your place?"

"Never!" The tea sloshed over the lip of the cup, and the attendant came forward with a cloth.

"Leave us," the king commanded angrily.

When the attendant was gone, he met Harron's eyes with a cold glare. "Is there such a child?"

"Yes, Your Highness, by some unfortunate miracle, the child survived and has come into my care."

"How can I be sure?"

"He is a striker, Sire, the exact replica of his father, your son. There is no doubt of his heritage. I have hidden him as long as…"

"Hidden him?" the king bellowed. "If you love your country, why have you not killed him?" The king's eyes narrowed. "Or perhaps, oh wise one, you held him in order to blackmail me?"

"It would seem there are arrangements that would be beneficial for both parties." Harron answered calmly. "You do not trust your son to rule in your place, and a grandson…"

"Silence! You are reaching for my kingdom itself." The king's expression was hard.

Harron waited in silence.

"I underestimated you, Harron." The king looked into the steaming tea thoughtfully. "So you want me to give you the kingdom? You are shrewd. That is a quality I respect. But," the king's eyes were on Harron once more, "you do not have the other qualities needed to rule a kingdom. I have already decided on my successor. When he returns from the battle, I will announce my decision. However, I will play along with your little game and give you a title and rich lands on the day the boy's body is delivered into my hands."

Harron's oily smile appeared. "You think me to be a fool, Sire? To kill the grandson of the king would make me the perfect scapegoat. When you killed me it would appease the kingdom of Oreathia and rid you of the threat caused by the boy. No, I will gain the title and lands and keep the boy as a promise to my safety. As long as my position and title remain, the boy's existence will be our secret. If at any time you attempt to remove me or lower my position, I will bring the boy into the public eye where he will quickly take his place as the ruler of your kingdom."

The king wavered, looking once more into the murky depth of the tea. "You drive a hard bargain, my counselor. However, contrary to what you may think, you do not have the upper hand. When Sir Rillian returns from leading my army, he will be crowned in my place by my decree. This much I can set right before my death. Deetry's foolishness has cost him the kingdom. Once Rillian is king, there will be no reason to fear the striker you claim to have found. If the people know I do not see fit to crown my own son, why would they even consider his unholy offspring as an option?" the king's eyes blazed with anger.

"Your Highness is upset. We will discuss this further in the morning." Uncle Harron's tone was as soothing as the fragrance of the tea. The king's passion had delayed the aroma's effect, but Harron could see it was beginning to numb the king's mind.

"You are no longer welcome here, Harron. Because of our past friendship I will allow you to leave Choi today. If you show your face here again you will be killed on sight."

Harron bowed slightly. "If it is what you wish, Your Highness."

"It is." For a moment the king's speech faltered. "I will have my chosen successor recorded before nightfall." King Deetrin promised, lifting the cup of tea to his lips.

Another bow and Harron crossed the room to the door. "I will leave you in peace." The law stated that if a king died without an heir and without naming a successor, the kingdom would pass to his advisor. If the captain outside did his job, the kingdom would soon crown Harron as their new king.

———————

The soldiers were closing in on Troy, ten against one. His

sword flashed in the softening sunlight, jabbing, thrusting, swinging but he was no match for the sheer number that was against him.

"Why are there not more soldiers to defend the prince?" Clance demanded, grabbing another arrow. The arrows flew from Clance's bow, felling Choian soldiers to the right and left of where Troy fought valiantly for his life.

"They were sent out yesterday," Jake answered. "News came of a convoy from an enemy nation that was headed this way. They went to meet them in battle to protect Choi."

"The prince did not accompany them?" Clance found it strange that an army would go out without their leader at their head.

"No, the king does not trust Deetry to lead his army. He cannot go himself so he sent them under the leadership of his most trusted knight."

Clance's arrow missed as his target lunged at Troy. Troy's face contorted in pain, but his blade never faltered and the man who had struck him fell to the stones.

The captain saw the wayward arrow strike the pavement. His eyes locked on the place where Clance and Jake were concealed. Moving to his right, he put Troy between himself and the archer, knowing the Oreathian would not chance hitting his own companion.

"Jake, you said once that you would give your life for your king." Clance pulled another arrow from his pouch. He had only four arrows left, and five soldiers and the captain remained. "You must put your life in danger for his sake now. Skirt around by the wall and get help for the prince if you can. If there is life in him, we must do all we can to save him. He will not last long unattended."

Jake scrambled to his feet and ran along the low stable wall. Sprinting across the open place, Jake continued on, keeping close to the shadows of the palace wall. Clance tracked his progress with an arrow ready on his bow. To his surprise, the big blacksmith from Choi rounded the corner, colliding with Jake. For a moment, Clance forgot about the battle. The boy was talking fast, gesturing towards the fallen prince. Clance watched as the big man, and a thick teen that closely resembled him, made their way around the battle to the prince's side. The Captain's back was to them as he watched his soldiers battle the enemy. Unnoticed in the commotion, the blacksmith lifted the prince and carried him inside the castle. A cry from Troy brought Clance's attention back to the fight.

———————

Jake pushed open the thick, wooden door and ran to the empty bed inside. Jerking the covers back, he made a place to lay the wounded prince. "I will find the physician," He called racing from the room.

Hans helped his father lay the unconscious body of their future king face down on the bed. "Move his head so that he can breathe," Ike instructed loudly.

Hans carefully turned Prince Deetry's face toward himself so that his ragged breathing would not be hampered by the pillow. Hans' own breath caught when he saw Prince Deetry's features. He stepped fearfully away from the bed. In the face of the prince, he saw Striker, older and yet the same, lying there cold and pale against the pillow.

"Striker is Prince Deetry's son." With wide eyes Hans turned to his father. "Striker is the prince of Choi."

Ike was busy trying to stem the blood flow without disturbing the arrow shaft that protruded from Prince Deetry's back. He gave no answer to Hans.

———————

Clenching his teeth, Clance put another arrow on the string. Troy had struck down one more disloyal Choian, but three remained, including the captain. He had risen to fight beside his companion only to be sharply commanded by Troy to remain at his post. Even in the heat of the battle, Troy knew that the striker would need to be protected at all cost. Clance knew that Troy would give his life to bring the striker to his rightful throne and save Choi. Sighting in on the nearest guard, Clance whispered, "Guide my bow, Almighty." before letting the arrow fly.

Troy was tiring, pivoting on his good leg instead of lunging to push back his foe, his stance was one of defense. When the man he was fighting dropped to the ground, Troy did not react. He simply blocked another blow, stumbling back under the impact. Clance knew they did not have much time. Did he dare to disobey his prince in an attempt to save his life?

The captain, standing just beyond Troy with his sword drawn, made no move to join the skirmish. As soon as Troy could fight no more, the captain would step in for the kill. Not daring to risk hitting his friend, Clance felled a soldier to the right who stepped back to catch his breath.

Two more arrows.

CHAPTER 19

Erastus shoved aside the heavy, false stone door that guarded the end of the tunnel. The clash of blades echoed loudly into the tunnel. Looking at the others, Erastus saluted Javen with the tip of his sword. "May the Almighty go before us."

Without another word, Prince Javen's protector sprinted from the tunnel into the courtyard to join the battle.

Javen felt cold fear gripping him. Long shadows were stretching their fingers toward the tunnel as if trying to grab and restrain him. Emmery put her hand on his arm, and he shook her off by habit without knowing he did. Sweat trickled down his back. Uncle Harron would be inside the castle. Though he was no longer a child, Javen feared Uncle Harron more than anything else in the world. Uncle Harron knew who he was and had no fear of hurting or starving the curse he had made the town promise to protect.

Emmery's voice broke through his thoughts. "You are not going into this castle as a curse, Prince Javen. You are the rightful heir of the king. Harron cannot take that from you."

———————

Hans stood at the door peering through the crack. He held a forbidden sword in his hand. A movement in the corridor caught his eye. Uncle Harron hurried past looking angry, yet pleased. He wore a leather bag on a strap across his chest. Glancing up and down the empty corridor, the old man did not see Hans through the thin crack of the door. He pulled something from his bag and dropped it into the decorative urn with peacock feathers pluming out of it. Straightening the feathers, he turned back the way he had come. Hans saw his cruel smile as he passed.

Moments later the physician arrived. The old man was out of breath. His eyes were red as if he had been weeping. Rushing to the Prince's side, he began giving orders at once. His supplies were soon laid out on a clean cloth on the bed. Jake arrived a few minutes later carrying a steaming pot of water. The water had sloshed out in his haste, leaving his hands red and painful, but his face was determined. Hans let him in and locked the door behind him. Jake's eyes were red and tears had wet his cheeks.

"What happened?" Hans asked going back to his task of tearing the bed sheet into bandages. At the bed, Ike's large, gentle hands steadied the unconscious prince while the physician carefully extracted the arrow.

Jake put the water where it was easily accessible to the doctor before turning to Hans. "The king is dead."

A shout echoed across the courtyard. The captain turned to see Erastus charging with sword drawn. Exhausted, Troy fell to one knee, allowing Clance the shot he had been waiting for. The arrow flew true, striking the captain between his armor just beneath his armpit. In shock, the captain turned toward Clance as his sword dropped from his hand. Clance's second arrow took down the soldier who was preparing to strike the fallen Oreathian with a death blow. Bursting from his hiding place, Clance raced forward, sword in hand.

The last soldier's face was dark with hatred as he drove his sword downward. Clance slammed into him, throwing the angry Choian off balance. The solider pivoted and dove at Troy once more. Troy collapsed to the ground causing the soldier's deadly thrust to fall short. With an angry yell, he jabbed again, his blade cutting deeply into Troy's arm. Erastus reached them a moment later, and the hateful soldier turned on him. Their blades struck again and again. Their skill was well matched, but Erastus was fresh and he drove the soldier back.

"They have shot Prince Deetry. Is Emmery with you?" Clance shouted to Erastus from Troy's side.

"She is here," Erastus answered, stumbling back under the force of the soldier's blow. He lunged, piercing the man's thigh.

"Why are you not defending your king?" Erastus demanded. He dodged and sprang forward. His blade flashed like lightening as he drove the solider back.

"We will have a new king soon," the man spat, breathing hard. "Uncle Harron will soon be king of Choi."

"You are wrong. Harron will never be king."

Their blades clashed together once more.

———

Glancing up, Clance caught sight of Emmery and Javen who stood a safe distance from the battleground. "Emmery we need you!" Clance called. "Prince Deetry has been badly injured. They have taken him inside through that door there." He pointed it out to her before turning his attention back to his wounded companion.

Troy's shirt was torn in several places, revealing the woven mail he wore beneath. Clance ripped a piece from the bottom of the injured man's shirt and pressed it tightly against the gash in Troy's arm. Grimacing, Troy held it in place while Clance tore another strip from the tattered garment. The ragged piece ripped in half when Clance tried to secure it over the wound.

Pulling out his knife, Clance would have cut a bandage from his own shirt, but Emmery stopped him. Kneeling, she produced several clean bandages from her bag of supplies.

"You must go to the prince," Troy begged, his teeth clenched against the pain.

She did not respond. Her hands moved quickly as she sprinkled dried herbs on the wound and wrapped it tightly with a clean piece of cloth.

Clance stood and scanned the area. Servants were peering out of windows and around corners, but no one came forward to offer their help.

"Watch out," a servant called softly. His eyes were on the wall above.

Clance looked up to see the gatekeeper's bow was drawn back to full strength. They were all fully exposed and well within the archer's range. Stepping between the archer and his fallen companion, Clance called up to him, "We ask for mercy."

The man looked down at them over his arrow. Clance wondered why he did not let the bowstring carry the blow of death. On his back were enough arrows to kill them all.

"The prince is badly wounded and we wish only to bring him healing if it is not too late." "I am sworn to protect my king." The gatekeeper's loud voice carried well.

"Then we beg you to allow us to help him." All eyes were on the archer above. He had the power to decide their fate.

"Kill us, we are soldiers," Clance offered. "Only allow this woman to go to Prince Deetry. She is a good woman and knows much of healing."

"I will do all I can for the Prince." Emmery rose with effort and shouldered her bag. "Thank you for understanding." Walking slowly, Emmery crossed the courtyard, knowing any moment the guard on the wall could take her life. No one moved as she ascended the steps stained with the prince's blood, and entered the castle.

"You did not kill the prince." The gatekeeper lowered his bow slightly. Slowly the tip of the arrow moved from Clance to the soldiers who still battled in failing light.

"Get away from him." The gatekeeper bellowed.

The swordsmen were too engrossed in their fight for survival to hear the command. From the archway, Javen watched as Erastus's sword struck again and again only to be blocked by the skilled fighter. Even Javen could see that the Choian soldier's reactions were not as quick. For one instant they stepped apart, both breathing hard.

In that instant, the arrow left the gatekeeper's bow.

CHAPTER 20

"Who is it?"

"Emmery. I was sent to help the prince."

"Who is it?" Ike's loud whisper filled the room.

"She said Emmery." Hans shouted to his father.

"Let her in," the physician answered before the blacksmith could. "She will be of much help."

The door was opened and Hans stood aside as the plump, stooped lady entered. She crossed the room to the bed without greetings. The doctor who was stitching up the damage caused by the arrow glanced up at her gratefully. "I am glad you have come."

"How is he?"

The physician paused for a moment. "I do not know if he will make it."

Hans and Jake glanced at one another. The doctor seemed to know and respect the oddly dressed newcomer.

"I have brought healing herbs." She set down her bag and looked at the boys for the first time. "We will need more hot water."

Hans unlocked the door once more. "Bring as much water as you can quickly carry. If there is not hot water, bring whatever water you can find and we will heat it here. You have built up a nice fire already."

Jake nodded and the boys left. Ike locked the door behind them and stood guard. He could see that he was no longer needed at the prince's side.

Erastus stood frozen as the Choian soldier fell dead at his feet. The shaft of an arrow protruded from the Choian's chest. As if in a daze, Erastus held his arm against his wounded side and looked around for the killer.

"On the wall," Clance called softly.

Erastus wavered unsteadily on his feet. Moving across the courtyard under the archer's arrow, Javen went to Erastus. The lean young man slipped a pale purple hand around the warrior's waist to support him.

"All will be lost if you are killed," Erastus warned, leaning heavily on him.

"You risked your life to care for me," Javen pointed out, straining to support Erastus' weight. "How could I not do the same for you?"

"Who are you?" The gatekeeper called down. The light was nearly gone now.

"I am Prince Javen, son of Deetry, son of Deetrin."

A murmur went through the servants. Many had seen their prince fall but now heard one in the darkness whose voice could have been mistaken for the prince himself.

"Light the torches," the gatekeeper commanded. Clance moved to Erastus' other side and together they pulled back to where Troy lay. The torches sputtered to life illuminating with long shadows the three brave men who had risked everything to save the king of Choi.

The chatter between the servants grew to an excited pitch. Many had known Prince Deetry when he was young. The boy before them was a perfect copy of their beloved prince. There was no doubt in their minds that Javen was the child of the missing princess of Oreathia, the beloved, forbidden wife of Prince Deetry.

———————

Uncle Harron sat in mock grief beside the bed of the dead king. The battle outside had ceased some time ago. Any minute the captain would be coming to give him the news. Prince Deetry had been shot, that news had already rippled through the castle reaching even those in the king's chamber. The door opened and a watchman appeared. He was of a lower rank and saluted Uncle Harron.

"Prince Deetry was injured in the skirmish," the watchman reported crisply.

"Injured!" Uncle Harron bellowed rising to his feet. He caught himself and quickly changed his tone. "Injured? How could this happen? Were your men not guarding him?"

"Sir, the battalions marched west yesterday to meet the rumored attack of the western allies. The king was warned that this would leave the castle at great risk of invasion."

"How dare you speak of the late king with such disrespect?"

The shock on the face of the watchman told Harron that the news of the king's death had not yet reached all of his subjects.

The pale man's gaze fell on the king, lying as if he were asleep on the huge bed. Silks and satins surrounded and covered him, yet the watchman could see there was no life in the king's lined face.

"Oh, my king, forgive me." He knelt without taking his eyes from the bed.

"The king was a person of great kindness. We will not question his actions while he was with us. The past cannot be changed. Instead, we will work as one to live up to the legacy he has left behind." Uncle Harron smoothed a wrinkle in the silk coverlet that draped over the edge of the bed. "Go, search out Prince Deetry and bring me news of his condition."

Nodding, the watchman rose and left the room. Harron saw the man wipe his eyes as he left the room. Loyalty for the royal family ran deep. Uncle Harron would have to be careful with his next move if he were to have the kingdom he desired.

———————

Emmery looked down at Prince Deetry. He lay unconscious, unaware that he was now the rightful king of Choi. To lose one's father without the chance to say goodbye is a hard thing to bear. "We must be gentle with him," Emmery spoke what they were all thinking.

Beside her, the physician nodded sadly. "It is an unthinkable tragedy. His Majesty was ill, but I saw no sign that death was so near."

Hans hung the poker on its gleaming stand beside the fireplace. "For being gentle, you certainly are being blunt about the news."

"Hans, your manners," Ike corrected loudly from the door. "I may not hear every word you speak, but your tone is not fit for the presence of royalty."

Embarrassed, Hans went to the door to stand beside his father. He turned his attention to Emmery and asked, "Would you permit us to go to the courtyard where the fighting was?" Seeing she was about to protest, Hans added, "You will have Jake here if you need anything."

This satisfied Emmery, and earned him an angry glare from Jake who wanted very much to go and see what was happening with the others.

"Very well, be careful," the doctor answered. Bring the wounded here and we will treat them. I fear there may be enemies even here in our castle."

Looking sour and disappointed, Jake took his post at the door. Checking the hall, he stepped aside to allow Hans and Ike to exit.

In their trips for water, Hans had passed the woven tapestry in the hall multiple times. For some reason, this time, the intricate soldiers caught his attention. It was a battle scene of soldiers with swords drawn as if going to meet a hated enemy. The weaver had done the scene well, and Hans could see the determination in their stances. They were there to protect their homeland or die. In that instant, the adventure was gone. This was not a game to play. This was the life of his country. This was the future of Choi.

CHAPTER 21

"You, on the wall, drop your weapon or the young prince dies." Laden's barked command brought instant silence to the happy chatter of the servants in the courtyard. The string of Laden's crossbow was drawn back, and the arrow well aimed at Javen's heart. No one dared to move.

"Drop it," Laden commanded once more.

The guard hesitated.

Laden turned with unexpected agility. His arrow struck the guard before anyone could move. The guard crumpled out of sight onto the parapet walkway, his bow falling with a sharp clatter to the stones below.

"When I speak, you obey," Ladan commanded, eyeing the crowd of castle staff who had gathered to see Striker, their prince. "If you speak without my permission, you will die. Oreathians lay your swords together on the pavement."

Erastus took Troy's sword so he would not have to rise and went to place it with his own blade alongside Clance's on the stones. As he watched the swords join his own, Clance felt a faint swell of hope. In his act of surrender, Erastus laid the swords so that their tips crossed one another. This was the Oreathian symbol of unity unknown to the Choian people. While they had breath, they were not yet defeated. Standing once more, Erastus looked past Laden and saw a rope hanging over the wall near the stables. That was how Laden had entered the castle. How wise of Harron to have arranged to have the castle emptied by creating a rumor of an attack. Now, the traitorous guards who were left to kill the prince lay dead or wounded. This gave Laden the opportunity to take control without opposition. Erastus looked Laden over critically, seeking a weakness in the cruel-faced man. The clothing of a farmer seemed out of place on the well-built assassin before them. He carried a full quiver of arrows on his back as well as a sword and a dagger at his side. His crossbow seemed to move as if it were an extension of his arm. Their only chance would be to be ready to attack if Laden faltered and gave them an opportunity to do so. Erastus glanced at Troy and did his best to convey a glimmer of hope. Instead, he saw the hopelessness he felt himself.

Laden had assessed the crowd and saw no one who posed a threat. "You, old man, Pick up the Oreathian's weapons and those scattered from the guards."

The stooped man's obedience was painfully slow.

Seeing fear in the faces of the people, Laden knew he was in control. He waited, toying dangerously with the crossbow, until the weapons were collected. "Now, walk them to the furthest corner of the castle," Laden instructed. "If they reappear, you will pay with your life."

The old man gave a little bow and, dragging the swords by their hilts, disappeared into the castle. The people were silent. Though he was no longer visible, they could hear the scraping of the metal against the stones as the old man carried out his instructions.

"Looks like I have chosen the perfect time to drop in," Laden was speaking now to Javen, who stood beside Erastus. "The guards are out and the castle is exposed to anyone who happens by. Uncle Harron planned it well, did he not?"

"What do you want, Laden?" Javen asked. As Striker, he had always cowered before this man. Now, as a prince, he felt no different. Only now, the people around him were his responsibility. They were depending on him for protection.

"I did not give you permission to speak," Laden answered darkly. His arrow was once more trained on Javen.

Javen's teeth clamped together. His eyes begged Laden for mercy.

"I am an assassin. I kill people for money," Laden told them loudly. "I will kill anyone who crosses me."

Several nodded fearfully.

"Striker, you have only these three fighting for you. They are wounded and tired." Laden paused to let the truth sink in. "You will come stand by me or I will kill the one on the ground."

Javen opened his mouth and shut it quickly. He had no choice. Laden would kill Troy as he had threatened if Javen did not obey.

"Javen, no." Troy's voice was so soft that Laden could not pinpoint who had spoken.

The sound of Javen's shoes on the pavement echoed loudly as he left the Oreathians to stand before his old enemy.

"News has reached me that the old king of Choi has died," Laden announced, removing the arrow from his crossbow and dropping it into his quiver. The young prince was well within range of his sword. The Oreathians had seen him kill the gatekeeper and knew there would be no chance of reaching Laden before he made his move.

Despite his threats, there was a low murmur of shock as those who did not know of the king's death came to grips with the grim reality.

"Your prince is badly wounded. There is little chance that he will make it through the night," Laden continued, slinging the crossbow strap across his chest so that the weapon rested on his back with the quiver.

Javen's eyes widened and he looked at Clance for confirmation. Clance's eyes were on the ground and his mouth was drawn into a thin line. Javen searched Erastus' face and saw no emotion there. It was as if the Oreathian soldier wore a mask to hide the turmoil inside.

"I want to see him." Javen's voice carried well in the stillness.

Laden's eyes narrowed. His sword was in his hand in an instant. The blade played in the air near Javen's neck.

"If you kill me, what will you gain?" The rush of emotions made Javen forget his fear.

"If I kill them, what will I lose?" Laden countered, cocking his head towards the Oreathians.

A quick murmur near the castle door drew their attention. There on the threshold stood Ike and Hans.

Laden's mouth twisted into an odd smile. "So the blacksmith joins the conspiracy."

"You will have to speak up, Laden. You know I cannot hear well."

Several hushed him with fearful glances at Laden, who in one fluid motion, was once again holding his loaded crossbow.

From the step, Ike could easily look over the heads of the others. "They say if I speak, you will kill me."

"What are you doing here?" Laden demanded.

"Do I answer him?" Ike asked Hans in his booming whisper.

Hans glanced at Laden, unsure.

Laden clamped his jaws to control his irritation. "Answer me, you fool."

"I was summoned by the King." Ike answered.

"You have the summons?"

"Of course." Ike pulled a crushed scroll awkwardly tied with a red ribbon from his shirt. "How do you think I made it into the castle?"

Hans' shock was obvious as he stared at his father.

"Let me see it."

"What did you say?"

With an exasperated sigh, Laden answered, "Put it away."

Hans quickly translated into his father's ear.

Ike obeyed, stuffing the document back inside through the neck of his shirt.

Once more, Laden's eyes played over the crowd. "You three by the door, high officials are you not?"

They nodded with obvious fear, and one opened his mouth to speak, but Laden went on without acknowledging their answer.

"Go inside the castle and open the treasury." Laden barked the order with no consideration of their rank. "You, stable boys, get me a wagon and hitch it to your fastest team."

They would have protested, but Laden's glare silenced them. That group by the door, you fill up bags of gold and bring them to the wagon. You have 30 minutes to empty this palace of gold. I have no need for trinkets, bring me the gold. Remember, the young prince's safety depends on your obedience. If you fill the wagon sufficiently, I will treat him kindly. If not, he knows what I will do."

Javen unconsciously shuddered, his face pale.

The chosen men hurried to obey.

"You there, page boy, tell Uncle Harron the people have gathered to crown him king." Laden smiled cruelly, his eyes hard. "You are to give him no other details or you will pay with your life."

The page nodded fearfully and ran to obey.

"Now we will wait, little prince, to see how much your people love you." Laden could see the boldness had drained out of Striker. "Did you really think you could be a king, Striker? You are no king, you are a curse. You are a freak of nature destined to bring pain and suffering wherever you go."

With his head down, Javen made no answer. The wagon was brought and the horses pranced anxiously, feeling the urgency of the grooms who held their bridles.

His mind drifted to what Erastus had said in the field years ago. "Rise above what they say. You are not what they say you are." Slowly Javen raised his eyes to look at Erastus. To his surprise, Erastus was looking intently at him, as if it was he who had reminded Javen of their conversation so many years ago.

Cocking his head slightly, Javen studied the soldier. He was not like the others from Oreathia. The difference was slight, almost undetectable.

Around them, servants were straining under bags of gold they carried to the wagon. They knew nothing about Javen beyond his relation to their king, and yet they were giving up everything in hopes of saving him.

Javen thought of the Widow Zina, she saw more in him than the curse. In fact, she did not see the curse at all. She saw him, Prince Javen, loved by the Almighty God.

When Javen looked at Erastus again he saw pleasure in his eyes.

Laden had not seen the exchange between the prince and his protector, but he had felt the boy stand taller beside him. Narrowing his eyes, Laden scanned the group in the flickering torchlight searched for the cause. His attention came to rest on Erastus who met his gaze without flinching. Unnerved by the confident almost triumphant look in the man's eyes, Laden turned his attention back to the wagon of gold.

"Your time is almost up," Laden bellowed. "Is that how little you think of your prince?"

"The treasury is far from this courtyard, we must travel…"

Laden shoved the man away, "I do not want to hear your excuses!"

The servant bobbed his head and ran to obey.

"You are getting ideas into that purple head of yours, Striker. I am warning you, if you want your friends to live you must obey me."

Prince Javen did not answer. The Almighty had given him value that could not be taken away. He watched the servants hustling to and from the open door. Beyond that door lay his father, a man he wanted to meet more than anyone in the world.

The page appeared and announced Uncle Harron was on his way.

"Clear a path for Uncle Harron," Laden commanded loudly.

Confusion broke out in the courtyard. The palace staff who were getting out of the way, collided with those transporting the gold to the wagon. A bag was dropped which, in haste, had not been tied securely. The gold spilled onto the stones, gleaming in the flickering light. Some dropped to their hands and knees to help gather it up. A hurrying servant tripped on one of them and his bag's contents flew along with him to sprawl on the unforgiving stones.

In the moment, Javen forgot himself and stifled a laugh. A traveling jester's act could not have been better than the antics of the scrambling servants.

Over all of the chaos, Laden was shouting orders that people were trying to obey.

Uncle Harron appeared in the doorway. A hush spread through the clamor of the courtyard. It was common knowledge at the palace that Uncle Harron was a person King Deetrith honored and expected his servants to honor as well.

"Laden, what is this madness?" Uncle Harron demanded.

"I am taking Prince Curse from the castle as ordered," Laden answered with the slightest bow. "Was there anything else you wanted done?"

"Me?" Uncle Harron took a step back, aware that everyone was waiting for his answer. He had fallen into Laden's trap. "I do not know what you are talking about. I have nothing to do with you kidnapping the prince. Let him go at once!"

Laden's smile was hard. "You, who raised the prince from

an infant without telling the king that his grandson was hidden in lesser Choi? Uncle Harron, honored guest of the king, who has been plotting for years for this day when you would take the throne from him?" Laden's gaze was cruel, "You let the crown slip from your grasp tonight, old man."

"Guards! Seize this man!" Uncle Harron realized as he said it that there were no guards. The people blinked at him in silence.

Glancing around, Javen suddenly realized that Erastus stood alone. Clance and Troy were no longer with him. In the confusion they had gotten away, but why had Erastus stayed?

Keeping a strong grip on Javen's arm, Laden jerked the prince along with him toward the wagon. "You had no intention of giving me what you promised, Harron," Laden informed him, "I have known that for years. But like you, I have a backup plan which does not involve you. You always wanted to be a hero, so I will give you a hero's death."

"How dare you make such accusations?" Uncle Harron glanced around for support. He saw by their faces that the people were undecided. "You are the one endangering the boy. I have been protecting him by order of King Deetry."

"Ha!" Laden looked into the wagon bed and turned on the servants who stood around, uncertain and afraid. "I see your new prince is not worth much to you. That wagon is barely full. I will return in a week and you had better have learned to care more, or what happens to the prince is on your own heads. As for you, dear uncle, I have a parting gift." He had dragged Prince Javen to the side of the wagon while he spoke. Taking a metal cuff from his belt, he deftly snapped it around both Javen's wrist and the bar of the wagon seat leaving the prince standing helplessly exposed as he turned to deal with Uncle Harron.

"Laden, no, we can talk this through." Uncle Harron had seen the cold hatred in Laden's face. "There are still riches for you."

"You did not listen to me when I advised you to make your move," Laden answered. He enjoyed making the old man squirm after pretending to respect him for so long. "Now you have lost everything and will pay for your mistake."

Uncle Harron turned to flee, but the assassin's arrow felled him on the same steps where Prince Deetry had fallen.

CHAPTER 22

"Only two more loose strings," Laden muttered. "Ike, step up here beside this traitor. I need you to secure him. Ike obeyed, swinging the pack off of his back to retrieve a rope from inside. The pack bumped against Erastus's leg as Ike let it down. Glancing down, Erastus saw Ike expose several intricate hilts inside his bag as he withdrew the rope. There was not room for a full sword, but Erastus could tell by the size that they were attached to good size blades. Ike propped the bag open on Erastus' right side and busied himself with his rope. Ike looped and fastened and pulled behind Erastus' back. Everyone could see he was tying a secure knot. Only those behind Erastus could see that the rope was not around the Oreathian's wrists at all. Instead, it was being held by the prisoner.

Confidently, Laden put away his crossbow and unsheathed his sword. "Had I more time, I would have loved to battle you myself," he said, allowing his blade to shine in the firelight, "You seem like you would have been a worthy opponent." He walked toward Erastus. It bothered him that there was no fear in the stranger's face.

"Often the Almighty grants us our desires when they align with His will." Erastus answered calmly.

Ike stooped to pick up his pack.

Laden rolled his eyes. "Are you foolish enough to believe…?" He stopped short. There was a glimmer of metal as Ike raised the pack to his shoulder. In that same instant, Erastus stepped back. A gleaming dagger of intricate design was in Erastus' unbound hand. The ropes, still knotted, lay on the stones behind him. "It seems you will have your desire fulfilled tonight."

Stepping back, Laden tried to make sense of the situation as Erastus moved forward to meet him.

"Have you forgotten, I have…?" Laden turned and froze. There, shielding Prince Javen, stood Clance and Troy. Both men held shortened blades of expert design. Behind them Hans was cutting the metal ring that held Prince Javen to the wagon.

"You have him no more." Troy pointed out. "Your battle awaits."

In desperation, Laden lunged at them in one last attempt to regain control of the prince. Clance surged forward to meet him. The length of Laden's sword made it hard for the Oreathian to do more than force Laden to keep his distance. He pivoted, racing around the wagon and clambering aboard. Grabbing the horse's reins, he slapped them hard, shouting at the horses. Spooked, they reared almost as one. It was this one moment of delay which saved Prince Javen. In it, Troy wrenched the twisted remains of the hated metal ring from Prince Javen's wrist, and he was free.

Erastus sprinted to the nearest torch. Jerking it from its stand on the wall, he hurled it towards the running horses. Because most of the horses had been taken to the battle on the western border, the loyal grooms had chosen young horses that were not yet fully trained in an effort to stop Laden. The horses shied away from the flames, and bolted. Laden tried desperately to reign in the crazed horses as the side of the wagon crashed against the stone wall that surrounded the courtyard. Wood splintered, and the front wheel gave way under the weight of the gold. The front of the wagon suddenly twisted downward as the wheel buckled. Laden flew from the wagon onto the hard stones. Everyone watched breathlessly as he tried to rise, only to sink to the ground once more. All around him, gleaming gold pieces littered the ground. His greed had become his downfall.

"You may come nearer," Emmery said softly as she beckoned Prince Javen to approach his father's bed. Even though Deetry was now the king, he remained in the common chamber. The physician and Emmery agreed that moving him would cause more damage.

Prince Javen nodded but did not move from where he stood. They said the pale face on the bed was so like his own. What if his father felt the same disdain the people of Choi felt for him? He had seen his father, but did he really want his father to see him?

"I must go and check on the Oreathians, will you be okay?" Emmery asked gently laying a hand on his arm. She handed him a damp, strong smelling rag. "It will help to remove the rest of the dye. I did not have time to make it in the tunnel. There is no need for you to be marked as something you are not."

Prince Javen took the rag and thanked her. Going to the mirror, Javen looked at himself for a long moment. Striker looked back at him. The uneven purple half of his face was all he had ever known. He looked at the warm rag he held. Could he really become a prince? Or was what they said true, was he an unwanted curse?

Someone cleared his throat at the door, and Prince Javen turned to see Erastus waiting politely outside the open door. The servants who guarded the room were looking to Prince Javen for permission to let him enter.

Embarrassed to have been caught before the mirror, Prince Javen looked away and fiddled with the rag. "Please come in."

"Perhaps it would be of more use on your face." Erastus pointed out.

Looking down, Prince Javen saw the purple of his right hand was barely noticeable where the rag had been on his palm and fingers.

"May I?" Erastus held out his hand, and Prince Javen gave him the rag.

"Emmery said it would help." Javen muttered, dropping his eyes to the floor.

Erastus put a hand behind Prince Javen's head to steady it as he applied the rag to the purple dye. "Close your eyes." He instructed, rubbing Prince Javen's forehead with the rag. "Have you spoken to him?"

"The king?"

Erastus paused, "Your father."

Prince Javen lowered his head, but Erastus gently tilted it upward again. "I am nearly done." The rag moved gently over Javen's closed eye.

"He has not awakened yet." Prince Javen answered softly, as if he feared his own voice would wake the king. "Emmery said he is badly injured."

"Yes," Erastus scrubbed in silence for a minute. "Does he know you are here?"

"I am afraid to speak to him." Prince Javen found it easier to talk to Erastus with his eyes closed. He could not see the room or his father who lay still a few feet away. Though he could not see him, Javen was painfully aware of the king's steady but labored breathing.

"There, see what you think." Erastus stepped aside to allow Prince Javen to see the mirror.

Though his face was rosy from the scrubbing and faintly

purple on the right side, it was clear that his own face resembled the face of the new king.

"Go and talk to him, Prince Javen. You do not know how much time you will have together."

Prince Javen went to the bed, with Erastus at his side.

Erastus was the first to speak. "King Deetry, your son is here. Prince Javen, son of Elise."

The king stirred, as if trying to awaken. The herbs used to ease the pain had put him into a heavy sleep.

"Elise passed into the world of the Almighty when he was born." Erastus went on, though the king still lay with his eyes closed. "He has been hidden away in Lower Choi by a man of great greed and ambition. The man is dead, and your son has returned to his rightful place at your side."

"Erastus, I think I should leave. If he does not..." Prince Javen fell silent as the king's hand moved across the comforter to weakly grasp his hand. His eyes traveled to King Deetry's face. His face was wet with tears. With great effort, the king squeezed Prince Javen's hand and whispered, "My son!"

Looking into King Deetry's eyes, Prince Javen knew that at last he was home.

CHAPTER 23

"They put Laden in prison," Jake announced, coming into the blacksmith's room without bothering to knock. "Laden will await King Deetry's judgment there."

"It is good news you bring to us." Ike observed from where he sat on the edge of the bed. "Laden is a bitter man with much hate inside." The blacksmith paused and added, "But even he is not out of the Almighty's reach."

"There is more," Jake went on importantly, "There is a rumor that King Deetrin was poisoned. They are holding a council in Prince…" Jake corrected himself quickly, "I mean, King Deetry's room." Embarrassed by his mistake, Jake fell silent.

"Father, one thing is still bothering me." Hans rose to pace the spacious room they had been given. He stopped to face his father and spoke loudly so he would be heard. "The gold is returned, the Oreathian's wounds are being treated, Uncle Harron is dead, and Laden is in prison. All this is as it should be."

Ike nodded in agreement. "What is bothering you, my son?"

"What about the summons? At the gate you said you did not have a summons," Hans scratched the side of his head trying to make the pieces of information fit. "At the gate you said you did not have it, but in the courtyard you did. How is this possible?"

Ike's booming laugh filled the room.

"When Laden asked, you had it," Hans pressed, "How did you get a summons when the king was already dead?"

Ike reached into his shirt and retrieved the small wax sealed scroll with its vibrant red ribbon. With a twinkle in his eye, he handed it to Hans. "Jake got it for me."

Jake, who sat across the room, grinned at Hans. "One of my better seal jobs." he boasted rubbing his nails against his shirt as if to polish them. "Even has real writing inside."

Hans broke the seal and unrolled the paper. Holding it up, he read, "Summoned by the Almighty." Han's looked up from the paper. "If Laden had read this, he would have killed you."

Ike rose with a grunt and took the paper from his son. "Perhaps, but the Almighty called me to come to the castle. I could not ignore His summons." He clapped Hans on the shoulder. "I am grateful you came along." Putting the paper into his shirt once more, Ike strolled from the room.

Jake sauntered over and draped his arm over Hans' shoulder. "I would give anything to have a father like that."

Hans grinned. "There is no one like him in the world."

———————

"It was the tea," Prince Javen insisted.

"You may not know this, but Uncle Harron often made King Deetrin tea." The steward pointed out patiently. "I have sent for the servant who was with the king when he died."

From the bed, King Deetry weakly nodded his approval. "We will not consider Harron to be at fault until proof can be brought."

No one missed the fact that the king did not use Harron's respected title of Uncle.

"The tea in the kettle in King Deetry's chamber when I

arrived, was a harmless blend of Chamomile," the physician pointed out as they waited for the witness to arrive.

"What made you check that?" The steward asked with a frown.

"When I entered King Deetry's chamber, I was aware of a peculiar smell." The physician explained. "When I found no mark on the king, I suspected poison to be the cause of his death and remembered the smell."

"Could it not have been my father's heart?" King Deetry asked softly. As much as he disliked Harron, he wanted to be fair in his ruling. Harron was dead and could not defend himself against their accusations.

An unpleasant look came across the face of the physician. "There was nothing wrong with your father's heart, Sire. Its weakness was invented by Uncle Harron. Your father was aging, but his heart beat strong."

"But the tea in his cup?" Prince Javen pressed. "Was it not the source of the smell? Troy told me there was a very strong smell when Uncle, I mean, Harron tried to poison him."

"The cup was empty. Some of the tea had spilled from the cup onto the coverlet, but it was just a little, as if it had sloshed over the brim when he received it." The steward responded.

The door opened and a servant entered, accompanied by a watchman.

"What is the news of the army?" Prince Deetry asked him solemnly.

The watchman stepped forward, "Sir Rillian's unit reached the castle a few minutes ago. I saw them thundering through the gate as we passed through the upper hall. The others are not far behind."

"Thank you, it is good news." The king looked over at Prince Javen, "Son, remind me to honor the page that rode to fetch the army. It was a wise move to do so without awaiting orders."

Prince Javen nodded, his eyes shining with happiness at being called "Son" once more.

"Now, for the account you bring," King Deetry turned his head on the pillow to meet the servant's nervous gaze.

"You are weary, Sire, perhaps we should…"

King Deetry lifted his hand to stay him and the physician fell silent.

"Thank you for your concern, but it is better to sort it out while the memories are fresh."

The servant shifted uneasily.

"You are Carson, are you not?" King Deetry asked.

"Uh, um, Yes, Sire." Carson faltered.

"Carson, you have served our family well for many years. You are not suspected of killing my father. We only want to know what you saw and heard."

Carson relaxed visibly. "I would not have left if I had known," he confessed, fresh tears springing up. "I loved your father, Sire."

"I know." Deetry's eyes got a faraway look. He too wished he had not left his father alone with Harron.

"What happened before you were sent from the room?" The steward, though he loved his king, was not an emotional man and was there for the facts.

"His Majesty was upset at dinner. A page burst in to inform the king he was in great danger, accusing Uncle Harron of a plot against his life. At that time, there was no proof to back his wild claim and the boy was sent away. I helped King Deetrin to bed and got him settled while Uncle Harron made tea. He has often made King Deetrin soothing teas, and so I thought nothing of it."

"Go on," the steward prompted when Carson hesitated.

"The tea had a very peculiar smell," Carson went on thoughtfully. "Uncle Harron said it was a new blend and promised King Deetrin would enjoy the flavor. I did not care for the smell of it and stepped back to get fresh air from the hall through the open door. Uncle Harron gave the tea to the king and they started talking in low tones. His majesty exclaimed, "Never!" with a dark, angry expression. In his passion, he spilled the tea he held. I went forward to clean it up and was immediately sent from the room. Uncle Harron came out a few minutes later looking both irritated and pleased. He hurried off down the corridor, and I returned to the king's side. King Deetry was clearly upset. He called for a scribe, but by the time the man arrived, the king had finished his tea and was quite calm and drowsy. He lay back and fell asleep." The servant choked up and could not go on.

Emmery, who had been silently listening from her chair near the wall, rose and came forward. "Your Highness, I took the liberty of checking Uncle Harron's bag when they carried him in. The herbs inside were harmless soothing teas that cannot cause harm on their own or blended together."

A quick knock on the door interrupted her.

By habit, the servant looked to the new king for approval before opening the door.

King Deetry nodded is permission.

Hans stood hesitantly in the open doorway, a bunch of peacock feathers in one hand and a small packet in the other.

"What is the meaning of this?" the steward demanded.

King Deetry and Prince Javen exchanged an amused glance at the sight of the peacock feathers pluming richly from the boy's hand.

"Forgive me for intruding." Hans bowed politely to the king.

"Come in. You have news?"

Hans crossed the room to the king's side, and laid the little packet on the bed beside him. "This is Uncle Harron's. I saw him drop it into the urn in the hall. The door was only open a crack and he did not know I was watching him." Han's realized he was still holding the feathers and looked around awkwardly for a place to put them down. Emmery came to his rescue.

King Deetry picked up the dusty packet and turned it over thoughtfully in his hand. "Is this the odor you smelled?" He asked. He would have held it out to them, but instead, he gave a little sigh and lay back on the pillow once more.

Prince Javen took the packet and handed it to the physician. He sniffed it gingerly and they could see the recognition in his eyes. The older man passed it to the servant who also confirmed the smell.

"You saw Harron with this packet?" the steward pressed, looking directly at Hans.

"Yes, Sir. The urn is just down the hall from this room."

Emmery and the physician were carefully examining the contents of the packet.

"I have never seen this blend, but I fear it is what was used to take the life of your father, Sire."

"If only there were more proof that it belonged to Uncle Harron." The steward spoke what they were all thinking.

"The peacock feathers are enough evidence for me." Prince Javen answered with a grin. "Surely you do not think that Hans would knowingly come to the king of Choi with a bunch of peacock plumes."

Han's could not help an embarrassed smile. "I forgot I had them in my haste to bring you the packet."

"Besides, I myself can confirm the packet belonged to Uncle Harron." Prince Javen went on. "I often saw him putting herbs into packages identical to this one. If you search the cottage, I am sure you will find more of that blend inside."

"The prince has spoken well," the steward observed. "The death of the king rests firmly on Uncle Harron and Laden who knew of the plot."

The others in the room nodded in agreement.

"It is decided." King Deetry spoke firmly. The scribe added a line with a flourish and began packing up his things to go.

"Now all of you must go and allow the king to rest." The physician ordered. "There will be time to arrest those, besides Laden, who were working with Harron and bring them to justice. King Deetry is badly injured and must rest."

As the others filed from the room, Erastus looked across the room at Prince Javen. The king's eyes were smiling as he looked up at his son. "I am proud of you, Javen."

Javen glanced up and met Erastus' gaze. Coming around the bed, he offered his hand to his protector. "Thank you, Erastus!"

Erastus folded him into a quick hug before holding the prince at arm's length as he had done in the woods. His eyes shone with happiness. "Now you will soar as you were made to do." Taking his once purple hand, Erastus once more placed the little wooden hawk into Javen's palm. "Farewell, Prince Javen of Choi."

———

King Deetry stood on the marble steps of the coronation hall. Though he had been king of Choi for several months now, the official ceremony had to wait until he had recovered from his wound. The crown was placed on his head and the great hall erupted with cheers. The people loved King Deetry. He was kind and good. The greedy laws that had come from Uncle Harron's advice over the years had been done away with, thus restoring Choi to a peaceful, prosperous nation.

King Deetry took his place on the throne, and another cheer went up as Prince Javen joined his father. He was seated in a smaller throne at King Deetry's right hand. Both were aware for a wistful moment of the absence of Elise, the beautiful queen of Choi. Even this wave of sadness could not quench the joy of the day. For on this day, Striker, the curse of Choi, was banished forever. In his place sat the beloved Javen, Prince of Choi.

STRENGTH OF SILENCE

Eddie stayed where he was, listening. In the distance, a motor started up. He waited until it had faded before he stood. Dizziness washed over him, and he steadied himself against the counter. Still moving unsteadily, Eddie removed the floorboards and laid them aside. He heard something out front and froze. If the police caught him here, there would be no end of trouble. Moving toward the back door Eddie pushed it open. Outside, trash cans and a variety of other things littered the yard. A car motor rumbled toward him, and Eddie ran.

JASON ROPER TRILOGY

Infused with invincibility and trained for greatness, Jason Roper is set to fulfill his father's dreams. But when Roper deviates from the instructions he is given, he stumbles upon an expansive criminal network. Determined to use his power to help those in need, Jason Roper discovers that there are times when invincibility alone is not enough.

Is Jason Roper destined for greatness as he has been told, or is his life just a front for a larger, more sinister plan?

THE MAN BEHIND THE MELODY

The unexpected death of his twin sister threw Mark into a whirlwind of change. Disowned by his stepfather, Mark set out with only one goal in mind, to get as far away from the hateful man as possible. He clung desperately to the last link with his sister, her saxophone. Wandering the streets, Mark's path crossed with a stranger who could see potential no one else could see. Mark, an unwanted orphan, was offered the chance to become more than he had ever dreamed. But could the stranger be trusted?

CARBON
AN UNFORGETTABLE ADVENTURE

Carbon slipped out of bed and turned on the light. Taking a sheet of thick drawing paper from her desk she drew the face of the man the article simply called Roper. Pulling the picture she had drawn earlier from her file box, she laid them side by side on the desk. It was little or nothing to go on. The prisoner could have been a thousand different people. She had no face to compare. Suddenly the image of the stranger in the alley came to mind and Carbon frowned thoughtfully. He was the only one who would know.

Taken by the Deep

"Must be a storm." Jeremy tried to sound confident.

"It's not a storm, Jeremy." Lydia's face was white and her voice faded into a whisper. "Please, you've got to let me go."

They didn't seem to hear her. Their eyes were riveted on the swirling water before them. It rose slowly as if the waves were standing, then moved forward with hypnotic swiftness.

Lydia screamed as the waters dove toward them. The salty spray

 wrapped around her, wrenching her from their grasp and pulling her into its depth.

Hodge Podge
Miscellaneous Stories for All Ages

A knight on a terrible mission, a stranger stumbling along the road, a faithful ship's captain, and a beautiful woman tainted by bitterness.

You will find adventure, danger, and fun filled entertainment in this random assortment of short stories for children young and old.

IN VISIBLE FEAR

Billy dropped back on the bed, flickering between the visible world and the invisible. His breathing was rapid and irregular.

"Keep quiet, Billy, and I'll do my best to keep them off your trail. They were asking about you today."

"Don't let them find me." Again, Billy grasped the man's shirt, terror in his eyes.

The dark man pried his fingers open and stepped away. "You keep your mouth shut, I'll do what I can."

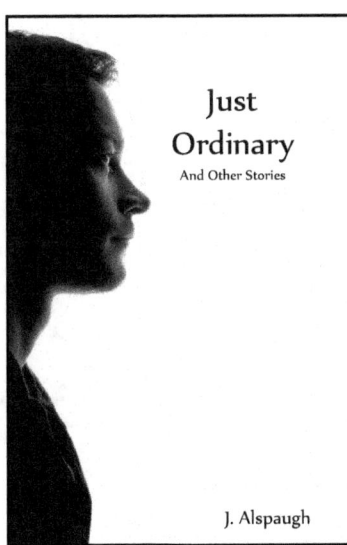

Just Ordinary
And Other Stories

Is there anyone who is truly just ordinary? Step into the world of fiction where heroes face mythical enemies, wrestle against enticing deceit, and battle fierce storms in a struggle for life. Experience heartbreak, adventure, and the ultimate sacrifice as you delve into the stories of *Just Ordinary*.